Bre

Am

methuen | drama
LONDON • NEW YORK • OXFORD • NEW DELHI • SYDNEY

METHUEN DRAMA
Bloomsbury Publishing Plc
50 Bedford Square, London, WC1B 3DP, UK
1385 Broadway, New York, NY 10018, USA
29 Earlsfort Terrace, Dublin 2, Ireland

BLOOMSBURY, METHUEN DRAMA and the Methuen
Drama logo are trademarks of Bloomsbury Publishing Plc

First published in Great Britain 2024

Copyright © Amy Kidd, 2024

Amy Kidd has asserted her right under the Copyright, Designs
and Patents Act, 1988, to be identified as author of this work.

Cover design by Publicis

Cover photo by Leo Byrne

All rights reserved. No part of this publication may be reproduced or transmitted in any form or by any means, electronic or mechanical, including photocopying, recording, or any information storage or retrieval system, without prior permission in writing from the publishers.

Bloomsbury Publishing Plc does not have any control over, or responsibility for, any third-party websites referred to or in this book. All internet addresses given in this book were correct at the time of going to press. The author and publisher regret any inconvenience caused if addresses have changed or sites have ceased to exist, but can accept no responsibility for any such changes.

All rights whatsoever in this play are strictly reserved and application for performance etc. should be made before rehearsals to Sovran Carey Ltd, Third Floor, 5 St Stephen's Place, Cork, Ireland T12 W84W (email: hello@sovrancarey.com). No performance may be given unless a licence has been obtained. No rights in incidental music or songs contained in the Work are hereby granted and performance rights for any performance/presentation whatsoever must be obtained from the respective copyright owners.

A catalogue record for this book is available from the British Library.

A catalog record for this book is available from the Library of Congress.

ISBN: PB: 978-1-3505-0813-2
ePDF: 978-1-3505-0814-9
eBook: 978-1-3505-0815-6

Series: Modern Plays

Typeset by Mark Heslington Ltd, Scarborough, North Yorkshire
Printed and bound in Great Britain

To find out more about our authors and books visit
www.bloomsbury.com and sign up for our newsletters.

ABOUT FISHAMBLE

Fishamble is an Irish theatre company that discovers, develops and produces new plays of national importance with a global reach. It has toured its productions to audiences throughout Ireland, and to twenty other countries. It champions the role of the playwright, typically supporting over 50% of the writers of all new plays produced on the island of Ireland each year. Fishamble has received many awards in Ireland and internationally, including an Olivier Award.

> 'excellent Fishamble . . . Ireland's terrific Fishamble' **Guardian**

> 'Ireland's leading new writing company' **The Stage**

> 'the much-loved Fishamble [is] a global brand with international theatrical presence . . . an unswerving force for new writing' **Irish Times**

> 'the respected Dublin company . . . forward-thinking Fishamble' **New York Times**

> 'when Fishamble is [in New York], you've got to go' **Time Out New York**

> 'that great Irish new writing company, Fishamble' **Lyn Gardner, Stage Door**

> 'the superb Irish company Fishamble' **Scotsman**

> 'Fishamble puts electricity into the National grid of dreams' **Sebastian Barry**

Fishamble Staff: Jim Culleton (Artistic Director & CEO), Eva Scanlan (Executive Director), Gavin Kostick (Literary Manager), Laura MacNaughton (Producer), Cally Shine (Associate Producer), Allie Whelan (Marketing, Outreach, and Engagement Manager), Emma Finegan (Literary Assistant)

Fishamble Board: Peter Finnegan, John McGrane, Louise Molloy, Doireann Ní Bhriain (Chair), Ronan Nulty, John O'Donnell, Siobhan O'Leary (Vice Chair), Colleen Savage, John Tierney, Denise Walshe

Fishamble is funded by the Arts Council, Dublin City Council, and Culture Ireland.

Fishamble's productions over the past decade include:

- *Taigh Tŷ Teach* by Eva O'Connor, Màiri Morrison, and Mared Llywelyn Williams (2024) in Kerry, and touring to Scotland and Wales, in partnership with Theatre Gu Leòr and Theatr Bara Caws
- *In Two Minds* by Joanne Ryan (since 2023) touring in Ireland and UK
- *King* by Pat Kinevane (since 2023) touring in Ireland, UK, Europe, and US
- *Heaven* by Eugene O'Brien (since 2022) touring in Ireland, UK, and US
- *Outrage* by Deirdre Kinahan (2022 and 2024) touring and online, as part of the Decade of Centenaries
- *The Pride of Parnell Street* by Sebastian Barry (2007–11, and 2022) touring in Ireland, and internationally, BBC Audio
- *The Treaty* by Colin Murphy (2021–22) in Ireland, Irish Embassy in London, and online as part of the Decade of Centenaries and Seóda Festival
- *Duck Duck Goose* by Caitríona Daly (2021–22) touring in Ireland, and online
- *On Blueberry Hill* by Sebastian Barry (2017–21) touring in Ireland, Europe, Off-Broadway, West End, Audible, and online
- *Mustard* by Eva O'Connor (since 2020) on tour in Ireland, internationally, and online
- *On the Horizon* in association with Dirty Protest, by Shannon Yee, Hefin Robinson, Michael Patrick, Oisín Kearney, Samantha O'Rourke, Ciara Elizabeth Smyth, Connor Allen (2021) online
- *Tiny Plays for a Brighter Future* by Niall Murphy, Signe Lury, Eva-Jane Gaffney (2021) online
- *Embargo* by Deirdre Kinahan (2020) online during Dublin Theatre Festival
- *Tiny Plays 24/7* by Lora Hartin, Maria Popovic, Ciara Elizabeth Smyth, Caitríona Daly, Conor Hanratty, Julia Marks, Patrick O'Laoghaire, Eric O'Brien, Grace Lobo, Ryan Murphy (2020) online
- *The Alternative* by Oisín Kearney and Michael Patrick (2019) on tour to Pavilion Theatre, Draíocht, Belltable, Everyman Theatre, Town Hall Theatre, and Lyric Theatre

- *Haughey/Gregory* by Colin Murphy (2018–19) in the Abbey Theatre, Mountjoy Prison, Dáil Éireann, Croke Park, and Larkin Community College, as well as on national tour
- *The Humours of Bandon* by Margaret McAuliffe (2017–19) touring in Ireland, UK, US, and Australia
- *Rathmines Road* by Deirdre Kinahan (2018) in co-production with the Abbey Theatre
- *Drip Feed* by Karen Cogan (2018) in co-production with Soho Theatre, touring in Ireland and UK
- *GPO 1818* by Colin Murphy (2018) to mark the bicentenary of the GPO
- *Maz & Bricks* by Eva O'Connor (2017–18) on national and international tour
- *Forgotten, Silent, Underneath*, and *Before* by Pat Kinevane (since 2007, 2011, 2014, and 2018, respectively) touring in Ireland, UK, Europe, US, Australia, New Zealand, and online, in English and bilingually in many countries
- *Charolais* by Noni Stapleton (2017) in New York
- *Inside the GPO* by Colin Murphy (2016) performed in the GPO during Easter, and screened internationally online
- *Tiny Plays for Ireland and America* by twenty-six writers (2016) at the Kennedy Center, Washington, DC, and Irish Arts Center, New York, as part of *Ireland 100*
- *Mainstream* by Rosaleen McDonagh (2016) in co-production with Project Arts Centre
- *Invitation to a Journey* by David Bolger, Deirdre Gribbin, and Gavin Kostick (2016) in co-production with CoisCeim, Crash Ensemble, and Galway International Arts Festival
- *Little Thing, Big Thing* by Donal O'Kelly (2014–16) touring in Ireland, UK, Europe, US, and Australia
- *Swing* by Steve Blount, Peter Daly, Gavin Kostick, and Janet Moran (2014–16) touring in Ireland, UK, Europe, US, Australia, and New Zealand
- *Bailed Out* by Colin Murphy (2015) on national tour
- *Spinning* by Deirdre Kinahan (2014) at Dublin Theatre Festival
- *The Wheelchair on My Face* by Sonya Kelly (2013–14) touring in Ireland, UK, Europe, and US

Fishamble wishes to thank the following Friends of Fishamble and Corporate Members for their invaluable support:

Alan Ashe, ATM Accounting Services, Dearbhail & Michael Bermingham, Doireann Ní Bhriain, Colette and Barry Breen, John Butler, Betsy Carroll, Breda Cashe, Maura Connolly, Jackie Cronin, Finola Earley, John & Yvonne Healy, Nancy E. Jones, Geoffrey & Jane Keating, Stephen & Susan Lambert, Damian Lane, Angus Laverty, Patrick Lonergan, Sheelagh Malin, Monica McInerney, Patrick McIntyre, Ger McNaughton, Anne McQuillan, Mary Monks Hatch, Liz Morrin, Pat Moylan, Ronan Nulty, Lisney, PwC, Tom O'Connor, Siobhan O'Leary, Andrew & Delyth Parkes, Judy Regan, Royal County Furniture, Jennifer Russell, Eileen Ryan, Colleen Savage, Catherine Santoro, Brian Singleton, William Smith, Eddie Soye, and Mary Stephenson.

fishamble.com   facebook.com/fishamble   twitter.com/fishamble

Acknowledgements

Thanks to the following for their help with this production: David Parnell, Liz Meaney, Bea Kelleher, Maeve Giles, Ciara Coyne, and all at the Arts Council; Ray Yeates, Sinéad Connolly, and all at Dublin City Council Arts Office; Sharon Barry, Ciaran Walsh, Alison Geraghty, and all at Culture Ireland; Ronan Nulty, James Kelleher, Karen Muckian, Kelly Corbett, Conor Leech, and all at Publicis Dublin; all at 3 Great Denmark Street; all at Fringe LAB; Willie White, Stephen McManus, and all at Dublin Theatre Festival; Emer McGowan and all at Draíocht; Collette Farrell and all at Droichead Arts Centre; Des Kennedy and all at the Everyman; all those who have helped since this publication went to print.

Fishamble: The New Play Company presents

BREAKING

by Amy Kidd

Cast

Sam and Charlie are played by Curtis-Lee Ashqar, Eavan Gaffney, Matthew Malone and Jeanne Nicole Ní Áinle.

Creative Team

Director	Jim Culleton
Set & Costume Designer	Alyson Cummins
Lighting Designer	Suzie Cummins
Music & Sound Designer	Carl Kennedy
Dramaturg	Gavin Kostick
Intimacy Director	Sue Mythen

Production Team

Producer	Laura MacNaughton
Production Manager	Eoin Kilkenny
Stage Manager	Steph Ryan
Marketing	Allie Whelan
PR	O'Doherty Communications
Assistant Stage Manager	Emily-Rose Champion
Chief Lighting Technician	Adrian Moylan
Wardrobe Supervisor	Maisey Lorimer
Sound Assistant	John Norton
Stage Crew	Damien Woods
Set Construction	Connach Production Services
Cover Artwork	Leo Byrne & Publicis
Rehearsal photography	Allie Whelan
Production photography	Anthony Woods
Associate Producer	Cally Shine
Executive Director	Eva Scanlan

Rehearsals were observed by Ad Astra students from UCD, where Fishamble is theatre company-in-association.

Breaking was first produced by Fishamble: The New Play Company, in the Dublin Theatre Festival 2024, at Draíocht and on tour nationally to Droichead Arts Centre and the Everyman. It was funded by the Arts Council.

Biographies

Amy Kidd is an actor and playwright who trained at The Lir Academy, Dublin (BA Hons, Acting). She is also a founding member of Anseo Anois Theatre, with whom she has worked primarily as an actor, but also as a collaborating artist on the writing and development of new plays and as a director (*Vanishing Grace, My First Breath*). Acting Credits with the company include: Sylvia in *The Pride* by Alexi Kaye Campbell, Alex in Wild by Jenna Kamal, Aisling in *Paler, Still* and Neesh in *Keeping Vigil*, both by Oonagh Wall.

Further acting credits include: Sarah Curren in *A Beauty That Will Pass*, Jess in *Love and Money*, Mary Shelley in *The Last*, Beatrice in *Inferno 21: Dante's Masterpiece Reimagined*, Sweetheart in *But You Stopped Their Hearts* and Young Woman in *You Can Leave At Any Time*. Screen acting credits include: *Bad Beat* (dir. Elena Walsh O'Brien), *Grind* (dir. John Francis Skally), *The Wedding* (dir. Fiona Stout) and *Short Stay* (dir. Ruth Meehan).

Breaking is Amy's debut play, she is delighted that Fishamble will be producing it's premier production under the direction of Jim Culleton and with such a fantastic team. She is currently writing her next play, with the support of Arts Council Ireland, The Abbey, Irish Theatre Institute and Fringe Lab.

Jim Culleton is the artistic director of Fishamble: The New Play Company, for which he has directed productions on tour throughout Ireland, UK, Europe, Australia, New Zealand, Canada and US, including eleven transfers Off-Broadway. His productions for Fishamble have won Olivier, The Stage, Scotsman Fringe First, and Irish Times Best Director awards.

Jim has directed for the Abbey, the Gaiety, the Belgrade, 7:84 Scotland, Project, Amharclann de hÍde, Tinderbox, Passion Machine, the Ark, Second Age, Dundee Rep, CoisCéim/Crash Ensemble/GIAF, Frontline Defenders, Amnesty International, Little Museum of Dublin, Fighting Words, Scripts, Dirty Protest, Draíocht, and Baptiste Programme. He has directed audio plays for Audible, BBC, RTÉ Radio 1, and RTÉ lyric fm.

He has also directed for Vessel and APA (Australia), TNL (Canada), Solas Nua, Mosaic, and Kennedy Center (Washington, DC), Odyssey (LA), Origin, Irish Arts Center, New Dramatists,

Irish Rep, and 59E59 (New York), as well as for Trafalgar Theatre Productions on the West End, and IAC/Symphony Space on Broadway. He has edited many books, most recently *Fishamble Tiny Plays* in 2024 for New Island Books.

Curtis-Lee Ashqar is a graduate of the three-year Bachelor in Acting (Hons) from The Lir Academy.

His most recent castings include Dave Hyndman in *Good Vibrations* musical at The Lyric Theatre, Belfast, directed by Des Kennedy. Prior to this Curtis-Lee and company won Best Production at Dublin Fringe Festival 2022, in Carys Coburn's *Absent the Wrong* at the Abbey Theatre on the Peacock Stage, directed by Veronica Coburn. After this, Curtis-Lee worked briefly with Druid, in their play reading series *Stars & Stripes*. Curtis-Lee also portrayed Hassan in *The DLO*, a play for young audiences crafted and written by Mary-Lou McCarthy.

Curtis-Lee has recently finished filming on *Blue Lights* for BBC NI. Other recent credits include the role of Xavi in the TV series *Hope Street* for BBC NI and on stage at Theatre Royal Stratford East playing the role of Laurence in the revival of Conor McPherson's *Shining City* directed by Nadia Fall. He has recently been involved in *Ourselves Alone*, a short film produced by Stockwell Studios.

He recently worked on a new play by Marina Carr, *Gilgamesh*, with theatre company Macnas playing the title role. Curtis-Lee appeared in the role of Jo in *Peat* by Kate Heffernan and directed by Tim Crouch at the Ark, Dublin.

Screen credits include roles in *Game of Thrones* (Season 5) directed by Michael Slovis, *Into the Badlands* for AMC, *Torvill & Dean* for ITV and the lead role of Ahmet in Murat Asker's short film *The Gift*. Some of Curtis-Lee's credits at The Lir include The Skriker in *The Skriker* directed by Tom Creed, Vaguin in *Children of the Sun* directed by Lynne Parker, *Three Winters* directed by David Horan, *The Garden* devised with Mikel Murfi, Damus in *Portia Coughlan* directed by Annabelle Comyn, the short film *Happyish* directed by Juanita Wilson.

Eavan Gaffney most recently played the role of Lusha in Rough Magic and the Abbey Theatre's co-production of *Children of the Sun*, directed by Lynne Parker. She performed in Emilie Hetland's

Revolutionary, directed by Katie O'Halloran, in *Staging the Treaty* written by Theo Dorgan and directed by Louise Lowe, and she played the role of Maud alongside Owen Roe in Sebastian Barry's *The Steward of Christendom* at the Gate Theatre, Dublin and national tour.

Eavan's further credits include *You're Still Here* by Murmuration for the Dublin Fringe Festival, *The Fabulously True and Timeless Tale of Sergeant Virgil* by Andy Crook for Faoin Speir.

Matthew Malone is an Irish actor. Named as one of The Irish Times' fifty people to watch, he has worked with many of Ireland's leading theatre companies. Matthew has been nominated by the Irish Times Irish Theatre Awards three times, including Best Actor for the role of Bernard in Philip McMahon's *Once Before I Go* (The Gate). Selected stage credits include *An Old Song Half Forgotten* opposite Bryan Murray at the Abbey Theatre, *Gold in the Water* (One Thousand Pieces | Lovano); *The Boy Who Never Was* (Brokentalkers); *Tarry Flynn* (Livin' Dred); *Faultline* (ANU); and the role of Gracie in Fishamble's *Embargo*. On screen Matthew recently appeared in Frank Sweeney's new film *Few Can See* (IFFR Tiger Award winner); and also played the leading role of Donal in *Dad* (RTÉ | Blue Ink Films) directed by Declan Recks. Further TV/film credits include *Miss Scarlet and The Duke* (PBS); *The Resistance Fighter* (Scorpio); *Valhalla* (Netflix); *Darkey Kelly* (Screen Ireland); and *As Luck Would Have It* (Zanzibar). Matthew is also a writer, currently developing a full length play funded by Arts Council Ireland and a new comedy-drama with support from Virgin Media. He trained in acting at The Lir, and also holds a degree in Drama and English from Trinity College Dublin.

Jeanne Nicole Ní Áinle most recently filmed a main role alongside Barry Ward and Charlene McKenna in the TV series *Clean Sweep*. Just prior they filmed the role of Dr Brady in the comedy feature *Apocalypse Clown* directed by George Kane.

In theatre Jeanne has just finished a run of *Metamorphoses*, written and directed by Jimmy Justice. Jeanne played the role of The Chorus in *Suzy Stork* directed by Ursula McGinn at Smock Alley Theatre, and the role of Grace in *An Octoroon* directed by Anthony Simpson-Pike for the Abbey Theatre.

Further credits include *Try and Touch*, directed by Nell Hensey; *Stay Alive* alongside Stephen Rea, Emmet Kirwan and Lisa Dwyer-Hogg, directed by Juliet Riddell; *Dungeons & Dragons* directed by John Francis Daley and Jonathan Goldstein for Paramount.

Alyson Cummins studied Architecture at UCD and trained at Motley Theatre Design School. She was a finalist in the Linbury biennial prize for stage design and has gone on to design for stage and television. Designs for stage include *Yeoman of the Guard; Acis and Galatea* (Opera Holland Park); *Scorched Earth* (Attic Productions); *The Pull of the Stars* (Gate Theatre); *In Two Minds* (Fishamble); *Volcano* – Best Set Design Irish Times Theatre Awards 2022 (Attic Productions); *The Race; Wires, Strings & Other Things* (The Ark); *Colic* (Hatch); *Morrigan* (Cork Opera House); *L'Amico Fritz, L'Arlesiana, Così Fan Tutte, Zaza* (Opera Holland Park); *Così Fan Tutte, Iolanta* and *L'Enfant et les Sortilèges* (Royal Academy of Music London); *Our New Girl, Medea, Jacques Brel is Alive and Well and Living In Paris* (Gate Theatre); *Last Orders at the Dockside, Heartbreak House, The Risen People, Quietly, Perve, No Escape* (Abbey Theatre); *Midsummer, This Lime Tree Bower* (Project Arts Centre/ Eoin Kilkenny); *Thick as Thieves* (Clean Break and Theatr Clwyd); *The Lion in Winter* (English Theatre Frankfurt); *Tosca* (Icelandic Opera); *Gulliver's Travels, Sinners, The Nativity & The Gingerbread MixUp, Mixed Marriage, Pentecost* – Best Set Design, Irish Times Theatre Award 2015 (Lyric Belfast); *The Nest* (Lyric Belfast/Young Vic); *Fabric* – Edinburgh Fringe First Award (Marlowe Theatre); *Macbeth* (Iford Arts); *The Lighthouse* (Royal Opera House); *The Night Alive* (DTF/Lyric Belfast); *Be Infants in Evil* (Druid); *It's a Family Affair* (Sherman Cymru); *Before it Rains* (Bristol Old Vic/Sherman Cymru).

Suzie Cummins is a Dublin-based lighting designer for theatre, dance and events. She has worked as a designer in Ireland for almost a decade. Suzie was the 2023 recipient of Druid's Marie Mullen Bursary, an award for female theatre artists working in the fields of design, directing and dramaturgy. Suzie was the associate lighting designer on the *Druid O'Casey Trilogy* in 2023. Lighting design credits include *Super Bogger, Danty Dan, Tarry Flynn, Trad* (Livin' Dred); *Lost Lear, The Wrens* (Dan Colley and Riverbank); *The Making of Mollie, The Race* (The Ark); *Absent the Wrong* (Once Off Productions); *Every Brilliant Thing* (Abbey Theatre); *After Taste*

(National Youth Theatre/Abbey Theatre); *The Secrets of Primrose Square* (Pat Moylan Productions); *Minseach* (Sibéal Davitt); *Before You Say Anything* (Malaprop); *Minefield, Charlie's a Clepto* (Clare Monnelly); *Harder, Faster More* (Red Bear). Associate lighting design credits include *The Giggler Treatment* (The Ark); *Party Scene* (Thisispopbaby); *Solar Bones* (Rough Magic).

Carl Kennedy is a composer and sound designer for theatre. He trained at Academy of Sound in Dublin. He has worked on numerous theatre productions, working with venues and companies including Fishamble: The New Play Company, the Abbey, Lyric Theatre, The Gate, The Gaiety, Landmark, Decadent, ANU Productions, Rough Magic, Theatre Lovett, HOME Manchester, Prime Cut Productions, Graffiti, HotForTheatre and Speckintime among others. In 2023 he received The Irish Times Theatre Award for Best Soundscape, and he also has been nominated three times previously in this category. He has made a number of audio pieces for installation and radio, working with ANU, Upstate Theatre Project, various museums in Dublin City and many others. He also composes music and sound design for radio, TV and video games. He was composer and sound designer for *Mr Wall* on RTÉJr which was shortlisted for an IMRO Radio Award in the 2018 drama category. Game titles include *Curious George, Curious about Shapes and Colors, Jelly Jumble, Too Many Teddies, Dino Dog* and *Leonardo and His Cat*. TV credits include sound design for *16 Letters* (Independent Pictures/RTE) and SFX editing and foley recording for *Centenary* (RTE).

Gavin Kostick, literary manager at Fishamble, works with new writers for theatre through a variety of courses, script development workshops and award-winning schemes. Gavin is also an award-winning playwright. His works have been produced nationally and internationally. Favourite works for Fishamble include *The Ash Fire, The Flesh Addict, The End of the Road* and *Invitation to a Journey*. Works for other companies include *This is What We Sang* for Kabosh; *Fight Night, The Games People Play* and *At the Ford* for RISE Productions and *Gym Swim Party* with Danielle Galligan in co-production with The O'Reilly Theatre. He wrote the libretto for the opera *The Alma Fetish* composed by Raymond Deane, performed at the National Concert Hall. As a performer he performed *Joseph Conrad's Heart of Darkness: Complete*, a six hour show for Absolut Fringe, Dublin Theatre Festival and the London Festival of Literature at the Southbank. He has recently completed a new version of *The Odyssey*, supported by Kilkenny Arts Festival. Gavin teaches at The Lir Academy and Trinity College, Dublin.

Laura MacNaughton has worked in the professional arts sector for over twenty years in theatre, film and dance. She has worked primarily as a general manager, producer and programmer. Laura has worked at a senior level in multiple arts organisations, these include The Gate Theatre, Dublin Dance Festival and The O'Reilly Theatre. She is co-founder and creative producer of Exit Pursued by a Bear, a theatre company for young audiences. Their first work *Our Little World* (2022), was commissioned in response to the impact of Covid on primary school children. Laura is a drama facilitator and director with Belvedere College Drama Department. She currently sits on the Arts Council Peer Panel for Theatre and the Producers Working Group for the Performing Arts Forum. Laura is the producer at Fishamble: The New Play Company and previous credits include *In Two Minds* (2023) and *Taigh Tỹ Teach* (2024).

Eoin Kilkenny has toured across Ireland and the world with theatre productions from Landmark Productions, Rough Magic Theatre Company, Fishamble: The New Play Company, CoisCéim Dance, Abbey Theatre, and many more. He has worked at some of the best festivals at the Traverse Theatre Edinburgh during the Festival Fringe, Galway International Arts Festival, Melbourne International Arts Festival, Dublin Fringe Festival and London International Festival of Theatre. He trained as a production manager with the Rough Magic SEEDs programme, working on their productions in Dublin, Belfast and New York. He is a product of UCD Dramsoc and has completed an MA in Producing at the Royal Central School of Speech and Drama.

Steph Ryan has worked in theatre for many years and with many companies including CoisCéim, Rough Magic, Abbey/Peacock Theatres, OTC and INO to name a few. Work with Fishamble includes *Handel's Crossing, The End of the Road, Noah and the Tower Flower, Spinning, Little Thing Big Thing, Invitation to a Journey* (a co-production with CoisCéim, Crash Ensemble and GIAF);

Mainstream, Rathmines Road, On Blueberry Hill, Embargo, Duck Duck Goose, In Two Minds and Pat Kinevane's *Forgotten, Silent, Underneath, Before* and *King*. Steph is delighted to be back working with Fishamble on *Breaking*.

Allie Whelan is the marketing, outreach and engagement manager at Fishamble: The New Play Company. Allie holds a BA in Drama and Theatre Studies from Trinity College Dublin. She has previously worked in marketing, social media and content creation roles with Dublin Fringe Festival, Poetry Ireland, Landmark Productions, Pan Pan, Glass Mask Theatre, The RDS Visual Art Awards and Music Network Ireland. She also works as a designer and photographer.

Cally Shine is a theatre producer from Seattle, WA, based in Dublin. She holds a BA in Theatre and a Minor in Irish Studies from the University of Montana and a Graduate Diploma in Cultural Policy and Arts Management from University College Dublin.

For Fishamble: *Duck Duck Goose* by Caitríona Daly (world premier and Irish tour 2021); *The Treaty* by Colin Murphy (world premier and international tour 2021); *Outrage* by Deirdre Kinahan (world premier 2021 and Irish tour 2024); *Heaven* by Eugene O'Brien (world premier, Irish tour 2022, Off-Broadway transfer and Edinburgh Festival Fringe 2023); *King* by Pat Kinevane (world premier, Irish tour, Edinburgh Festival Fringe 2023, and North American tour 2024); *The Humours of Bandon* by Margaret McAuliffe (North American tour 2023).

For Once Off Productions: *Rescue Annie* by Eoghan Carrick and Lauren Shannon Jones (Dublin Fringe Festival 2021); The Performance Corporation's *Emperor 101* (Dublin Theatre Festival 2021); *Looking For América* by Federico Julián González and Janet Moran (Edinburgh Festival Fringe 2021, and Irish tour 2022); *Absent the Wrong* by Carys D. Coburn (winner Best Production, Dublin Fringe Festival 2022); *Quake* by Janet Moran (Dublin Theatre Festival 2023, Zebbie Award nominee 2024); *The United States v. Ulysses* by Colin Murphy (world premier 2023, Zebbie Award nominee 2024); *You Belong To Me* by Rory Nolan (world premier 2023); *Elsewhere* by Michael Gallen (Irish tour 2024);

Afterwards by Janet Moran (Dublin Fringe Festival 2024); *Guest Host Stranger Ghost* by Kate Heffernan (Dublin Theatre Festival 2024).

For Dead Centre: *Chekhov's First Play* by Dead Centre (international tour 2022).

Eva Scanlan is the executive director at Fishamble: The New Play Company. Current and recent producing work includes *Taigh Tŷ Teach,* a trilingual co-production with partners in Scotland and Wales, *In Two Minds* by Joanne Ryan, *Heaven* by Eugene O'Brien, *Outrage* by Deirdre Kinahan, *The Treaty* by Colin Murphy, *Embargo* by Deirdre Kinahan, *The Alternative* by Michael Patrick and Oisín Kearney, *On Blueberry Hill* by Sebastian Barry, Fishamble's award-winning plays by Pat Kinevane *King, Before, Silent, Underneath* and *Forgotten,* and many other productions on tour in Ireland and around the world.

Eva produces *The 24 Hour Plays: Dublin* at the Abbey Theatre in Ireland (2012-present), in association with the 24 Hour Play Company, New York as a fundraiser for Dublin Youth Theatre. She has worked on *The 24 Hour Plays* on Broadway and *The 24 Hour Musicals* at the Gramercy Theatre in New York. Previously, she was Producer at terraNOVA Collective in New York (2012–15) and has worked on events and conferences at the New School, the Park Avenue Armory and Madison Square Garden.

Breaking

Notes on the play

This is a full-length play, in two acts.

In the original production the cast was as follows:

Eavan Gaffney

Curtis-Lee Ashqar

Jeanne Nicole Ní Áinle

Matthew Malone

In **Act One** *the character of* **Sam** *was played by* **Matthew Malone** *and* **Jeanne Nicole Ní Áinle**, *and the character of* **Charlie** *was played by* **Curtis-Lee Ashqar** *and* **Eavan Gaffney**.

Cast should play in their own gender, their natural accent and as the age they appear to be.

I believe it serves the presentation of this text for each actor to be from a different cultural background and/or of a different race where possible i.e. perhaps . . . a Black actor, a White actor, an Asian actor and a Middle Eastern actor. You might also choose to explore other differences: age gaps, class differences, city vs rural, etc.

You may choose to disregard some or all of these suggestions. That's okay. You are free to do so, and you are also free to present the play with a larger or smaller cast, if you wish. The exploration of gender, race, sexuality and any other aspect of our differences, should be led by curiosity and not seeking to provide an answer or to make a particular point.

As an example, here is how casting played out in the original production . . .

Act One

Scene 1: Sam – Matthew	Charlie – Curtis-Lee
Scene 2: Sam – Matthew	Charlie – Curtis-Lee/Eavan
Scene 3: Sam – Matthew/Jeanne	Charlie – Eavan
Scene 4: Sam – Jeanne	Charlie – Curtis-Lee
Scene 5: Sam – Matthew	Charlie – Curtis-Lee
Scene 6: Sam – Matthew	Charlie – Eavan
Scene 7: Sam – Jeanne	Charlie – Curtis-Lee

This is merely one option. I recommend exploring each scene with each possible combination of your cast of actors, then decide what you would like to present to your audience, based on this. What will be most compelling for one company's production and cast, may be very different to another company's production with a different cast.

/ – an interruption

. . . – an ellipses as a stand-alone line indicates a particularly active unspoken thought/non-verbal communication, which will most likely elicit a shift in the breath

Act One

Scene One

Sam's apartment. Mid-morning.

Sam *sits at a desk working on a laptop, surrounded by papers and books.*

Charlie *emerges from the bedroom, not long awake, and stands in the doorway a moment, watching* **Sam** *at work.*

Charlie Sam.

Sam *continues to work.*

Charlie Sam.

Sam *continues to work.*

Charlie Sammy . . .

Sam.

Sam Mmhmm.

Charlie Sam.

Sam Yeah, Charlie. I said yeah.

Charlie Do you still love me?

Pause.

Sam Yes.

Charlie Yeah. You sure?

Sam Yes, Charlie.

Charlie Good.

Pause.

Are you reeeaally / sure –

Sam Charlie, I'm working. I'm at work right now.

Charlie Sorry.

Charlie *moves over to the sofa, where they've left their iPad and headphones and lies down, sprawling out and stretching.* **Charlie** *puts the headphones on but the headphone jack dangles absent-mindedly as they search on YouTube and select a video.*

Charlie *presses play on the video.*

Still not noticing that the headphones aren't plugged in, **Charlie** *increases the volume.*

Some time passes.

Sam You know those headphones aren't plugged in.

Charlie, *attention on the video, hasn't heard this. Laughs at the screen.*

Sam Could you maybe turn it down a bit?

Charlie Huh?

Charlie *finally notices that the headphones are dangling –*

Oh! Ha.

– plugs them in and continues enjoying the video.

Pause.

Sam When do you leave for work?

Pause.

Charlie.

Pause.

(*Louder.*) Charlie, when are you leaving?

Charlie *pauses the video and removes the headphones.*

Charlie What, Sammy?

Sam Errr. When are you off to work?

Charlie Oh. Two thirty, two forty-five ish.

Sam *checks the time.*

Sam Right.

Pause. They smile at each other.

Charlie *is about to return to the video, when –*

Sam I wish you wouldn't ask me that all the time.

Charlie Ask you what?

Sam If I love you.

Charlie If you said it more I wouldn't have to.

Sam I tell you I love you all the time.

Charlie I tell you I love you more.

Sam That's – I say it a normal amount.

Charlie So, what? I love you too much?

Sam That's not – no. Just – I – ah. Never mind.

Charlie You're pretty mean to me, sometimes. But I do love you.

Sam . . . No, I'm not?

Charlie Only joking.

Sam Okay. I don't think I . . . I mean, I'm sorry. If you feel like I . . .

Charlie Go on, get back to work. You're cute when you're concentrating.

Sam *half turns back to their work. Suddenly remembers –*

Sam Wait. But I thought you were working a mid-shift today?

Charlie Half three till close.

Sam I thought – I'm sure you said it was earlier?

Charlie Nope, half three till close.

Sam Right . . .

Charlie Why? You want to get rid of me?

Sam No, no. I just – I thought that was why you had to stay over last night.

Charlie I didn't have to, I wanted to spend time with you.

Sam I really do have to get this done today.

Charlie Finish it when I go in.

Sam It doesn't really work like that.

Charlie You're freelance, it doesn't matter when you do it as long as it's done.

Sam Maybe that's . . . technically true. But . . . Well, just because I *can* work any time doesn't mean I want to. I like routine and structure and – solitude. I work better when I work under the right circumstances.

Time of day, environment. It all makes a really big difference.

Charlie That sounds like a lot of fancy ways of saying 'fuck off Charlie'.

Sam No, no! Honestly, I promise.

Charlie You could take a long lunch. From now until I go. Then work a couple of extra hours this evening. You'll still get it all done.

Sam I want to do it now. My . . . my brain's used to working / at this –

Charlie That's in your head, you know.

Sam Yes, actually. It is. It's psychology. Science. And it's evidence based.

My energy is better now. I've done my morning routine, I've done my starting rituals and all of that tells my brain that, that it's / time to –

Charlie Sounds like a load of shit.

Sam It helps me.

Charlie Just do all that on the days that I'm not here, then.

Sam You're always here.

Charlie Start it when I go to work.

Sam I work best in the mornings –

Charlie Do it when I'm at mine.

Sam My work is important to me, Charlie –

Charlie You just don't want to spend time with me.

Sam – and you're never at yours anymore.

Pause.

Charlie Is that a problem?

Pause.

Sam No.

Pause.

Charlie Have I annoyed you?

Sam No.

Charlie I have.

Sam No, no, you're fine.

Charlie I have. I have, I've annoyed you. Great. Sorry.

Sam No, please don't get upset. I'm sorry.

Pause.

I'm sorry, Charlie.

Charlie.

You haven't annoyed me.

Come here.

Charlie *comes to* **Sam**.

10 Breaking

Sam *embraces* **Charlie**.

Sam I'm sorry if I hurt your feelings. I love you.

Charlie I love you too, Sammy Sam.

They embrace for a moment. Then –

I've got an idea!

Sam Charlie, I really do need to –

Charlie No, no, no, shush. Ssssh. Here. Look. Let's put this away. Please.

Charlie *shuts the laptop.*

Sam Charlie!

Charlie Please, Sam. Don't argue. Please. No more arguing.

Just this once? Please. Please . . .?

Look, you deserve a break! And I am – I'm being a pain in the arse and I'm going to make up for it. It's not going to happen every day, but just for today, please, I want to make it up to you. I want to. I want to . . . make you a great-big-fuck-off-brunch.

Sam Charlie, I don't . . .

Charlie Sam. I insist. I was being annoying, I get it. I know. I was being . . . I've been hanging about all day, lounging around in your apartment, making a mess, taking up space, doing sweet fuck all and the absolute least I can do is treat you to a nice meal once in a while.

Right? So. What have you got in?

Sam Umm –

Charlie Eggs? Have you got eggs?

Sam *nods.*

Charlie Good. Tomatoes? Avocado?

Act One, Scene One   11

Sam   Yeah.

Charlie   And your favourite – smoked salmon?

Sam   There's a bit left in that pack, yeah. Not much. But –

Charlie   Well, I'll put the salmon in yours then, yeah?

I'll cook it right into the scrambled eggs, just the way you like it. Yeah?

Sam   Thanks.

Charlie   Why don't you nip over to that place you love, the one across the road? Get us some proper coffees to have with it. You'd like that wouldn't you? And get some air. I think some air would do you good, wouldn't it? And I'll get cooking.

Sam   Yeah. Okay. But – . . . Okay.

Charlie   Okay. Coat.

Charlie *holds out the coat and helps* **Sam** *into it.*

Sam   Thanks.

Charlie   Kiss?

They kiss.

Love you.

Sam   I love you too.

Charlie   Oat milk cappuccino.

Sam   I know.

Sam *leaves.*

Scene Two

Sam's apartment. The early hours of the morning.

Sam *and* **Charlie** *were out with friends tonight. They are very drunk. Music plays.*

They dance together. Then, **Charlie** *breaks away and stumbles to the sofa. Drinks.*

Sam *keeps dancing.* **Charlie** *keeps drinking, watching* **Sam***.*

After some time, **Charlie** *stands again, wobbly, moving over to* **Sam** –

Charlie   I fucking love you.

Sam   I fucking love you.

Charlie *kisses* **Sam***.*

Charlie   You look amazing when you dance.

Sam *kisses* **Charlie***.*

Charlie   Majestic.

Sam *laughs.*

They kiss.

They wind their way back to the sofa, entangled.

The song comes to an end.

Sam   Where did the music go?

Charlie   Song finished.

Sam   But why did it stop?

Charlie   I said it ended, silly.

Sam   It's on a playlist though.

Charlie   Oh . . . Don't know then.

They laugh. They kiss.

Charlie You look great.

Sam You look great.

Charlie No, seriously, you look . . .

Hey, why did you have that big jumper on all night?

Sam I don't know. It's comfy and I was a bit cold. Why?

Charlie You should show off your body more when we go out.

Sam (*laughing*) Stop it. No, don't be silly.

Charlie I'm not, I'm serious. I love your body. You look . . .

Sam Great? You said that already.

Charlie I want everyone to see how lucky I am.

Sam Oh yeah?

Charlie Yeah. I'm going to dress you next time we go out. Alright?

Sam Dress me? You're going to dress me up like a doll?

Charlie Let me. Go on, it'll be fun.

Sam Dress me how?

Charlie Something tight. Something sexy. I want to show you off.

Sam That's not really me, Charlie . . .

Charlie It'll be fun.

Sam Okay, maybe. If you insist.

Charlie Tonight was fun.

Sam Yeah, it was.

Charlie Frankie was in good form.

Sam Yeah.

Charlie I thought we got on well tonight.

Sam Me and you?

Charlie Me and Frankie.

Sam Oh. Yeah. Maybe.

Charlie Didn't you think?

Sam I didn't really notice either way, I wasn't paying much attention to Frankie.

Charlie Usually we don't.

Sam Get on?

Charlie No. I made a joke and Frankie laughed. At the bar.

Sam That's nice.

Charlie Yeah, it was good I think.

Sam I think you're overthinking it.

Charlie I'm saying it's a good thing.

Sam You're always thinking that you don't get on with people. Always thinking / that people don't like –

Charlie / Well, people don't like –

Sam – you! See!

Charlie They don't. Frankie doesn't.

Sam But, you just said –

Charlie Frankie likes you.

Sam Well, Frankie's my friend.

Charlie Frankie fancies you.

Sam Ugh, no. No. Shut up.

Charlie Of course Frankie fancies you, everyone fancies you.

Sam They don't.

Charlie But I get to have you.

Charlie *kisses* **Sam**.

Charlie More wine?

Sam Yeah. Thanks.

Charlie Uh-oh. Empty.

Sam Already. That was quick.

Charlie There's another bottle.

Sam Is there?

Charlie Yeah, we got one on the way home.

Sam Oh, yeah!

Charlie Go get the other bottle.

Sam Where is it?

Charlie Bedroom.

Sam Why's it in the bedroom? Where?

Charlie In my bag, remember?

Sam Oh. Right. Which bag?

Charlie Never mind. I'll get it.

Charlie *exits through the bedroom door.* **Sam** *sinks further into the sofa, drunkenly.* **Sam** *yawns, sleepiness setting in.*

Charlie *returns, triumphantly, with the new bottle of wine – makes a show of opening it and pouring out the two glasses, passing one to* **Sam**.

Sam Thank you.

They drink.

Charlie You should dance again.

Sam There's no music.

Charlie Dance for me.

Sam Don't want to. I'm tired.

Charlie Alright.

Sam And my neck's all achy.

Charlie Again?

Sam I know. I keep straining it.

Charlie Well, you're always –

Sam Hunching over my laptop. Yeah, yeah, I know. I know.

Charlie Poor Sammy. You want a massage?

Sam Mmm, please. Yeah. In the morning. Too tired now.

Charlie No. Don't get sleepy yet.

Sam We've been up for hours.

Charlie But we haven't . . . *you know* . . . yet . . .

Sam Don't know if I want to.

Charlie Ah, that's not fair. You've got me in the mood.

Sam Oh yeah?

Sam *kisses* **Charlie**.

Charlie See, you do want to.

Sam No, I'm too tired. Maybe in a bit.

Charlie You'll fall asleep.

Sam I'm too drunk.

Charlie I just opened another bottle of wine.

Sam Sorry.

Charlie What do you want to do then?

Sam Cuddle.

Charlie Yeah?

Sam Talk.

Charlie What about?

Sam Something nice.

Charlie Something nice . . .

Sam Or. Tell me something you haven't told me before.

Charlie Hmmm . . . I love you?

Sam (*fake snore*) Boring. You're a broken record.

Charlie *laughs.*

Sam *snuggles into* **Charlie**'s *chest.* **Charlie**'s *arm wraps around.*

Charlie Hmmm . . .

Something else . . .

Pause. **Sam** *snuggles further in, eyes closing.*

Long pause.

And then . . .

Charlie When I was nine a kid in my class cornered me in the playground – called me all these names – and I pissed myself. And everyone saw.

Pause.

Sam's *eyes open.*

Sam Really?

Charlie Really.

It's not something nice, but it is something I haven't told you before.

Sam Why did they do that?

Charlie   I don't know. I didn't get on with other kids. They thought I was weird.

Sam   I'm sorry that happened to you.

Charlie   It's okay.

Sam   I love you.

Charlie   I love you too.

Pause.

Sam *snuggles back into* **Charlie**, *closing their eyes again.*

Sam   My mum* used to call me names.

Charlie   I know.

Pause.

Sam   She didn't mean it though.

Charlie   I know.

Pause.

Are you falling asleep?

Pause.

Sam?

Pause.

Sammy?

Sam   Hmm?

Charlie   Are you falling asleep?

Pause.

Sam *is asleep.*

* **'Mum'** *should be changed to 'Mam', 'Mom' etc according to what is natural for the actor.*

Scene Three

Sam's apartment. Day.

An empty stage. Then – a knock at the door.

Sam *enters from the bedroom and rushes to open it. It's* **Charlie**. *They embrace.*

Sam Oh, thank God!

Charlie Hey! Hey you!

Sam Thank God you're here, thank you. Thank you for coming.

Charlie Of course I came.

Sam I missed you.

Charlie I missed you too, so much. Are you okay now?

Sam Better, a bit better.

Charlie Good. Good. I was so worried about you. Here, sit down. Or, or lie.

Sam I'm feeling a lot better.

Charlie Good, but still. Relax. I want to look after you. Lie down here.

Sam Okay.

Charlie So what happened?

Sam I just got really faint, dizzy, and I thought I was going to be sick.

Charlie God.

Sam I wasn't though.

Charlie Good.

Sam But I just had to sit down. Right there in the, fucking, canned foods aisle. My knees went completely weak, and everything was spinning. So, I grabbed on to the trolly to, to steady myself – stupid – but the wheels were – you know – obviously – so. I just sat down. On the floor. In the aisle. Oh God, it was so embarrassing.

Charlie As long as you're alright.

Sam Yeah, right.

Charlie Have you drunk enough water? Since?

Sam Mmm. A bit. Probably not enough.

Charlie I'll get you some.

Sam I have a bottle by my bed, I'll get it.

Charlie I'll get it.

Sam I can get it, Charlie. But, thank you.

Sam *goes into the bedroom.*

Sam *returns with a bottle of water.*

Charlie Drink.

Sam I will.

Charlie Drink now.

Sam Okay, okay, drinking.

Sam *drinks.*

Thanks.

Sam *sits.*

Charlie So what happened after you sat down in the aisle?

Sam Someone asked me if I was okay. But I couldn't get any words out and then they – I think they went and got someone – a member of staff.

Charlie Right.

Sam Maybe they didn't get them, maybe the other person – the member of staff – maybe they were just in the aisle too. I was a bit out of it.

Act One, Scene Three

Charlie Yeah, of course.

Sam Anyway, they took me to the back, and I sat on a barrel thing for a bit.

Charlie Okay.

Sam No, not a barrel, a . . . a crate?

Charlie A crate, right, yeah.

Sam With my head between my legs.

Charlie Nice.

Sam Texted you –

Charlie Yeah.

Sam – as soon as I could focus on the screen properly. It, it wasn't so blurry then but I was still sure I was going to get sick. Everything was so, you know –

Charlie Poor Sammy.

Sam Anyway, because I could – you know – I was actually able to function a bit more at this point – able to use my phone at least – so, I got a taxi, on the app. I thought I was gonna throw up in the car. Get a fine.

Charlie God, yeah. Last thing you need. You poor thing.

Pause.

And you think it was a . . .?

Sam Yes. Yep. Just . . . just a panic attack, I think.

Charlie Like you . . .

Sam Like the ones I used to have. The ones I told you about. Yes.

Charlie And you're sure?

Sam So embarrassing.

Charlie You're sure we don't need to go to the hospital or anything? Just to be safe?

Sam I'm sure.

Charlie Okay.

Sam Once I got home and lay down for a bit it passed.

Charlie Good. I'm glad. I was so worried.

Sam I'm sorry that I worried you.

Charlie It's okay. I'm sorry I wasn't here sooner. I got here as fast as I could, but it's a long –

Sam I know. Yeah. You were right, getting in from yours is . . .

Charlie Yeah.

Sam Yeah.

Pause.

And – about that, actually . . . Errr. I actually . . .

I did want to talk to you about how we left things the other day.

I'm sorry. What I said wasn't fair.

Pause.

You were totally right. I have this lovely flat right in the centre and your place is . . . yeah . . . and with everything that's going on with your housemates at the moment, it's . . . Well, I get it.

Charlie Yeah?

Sam Yes, of course. Of course you can stay here. Whenever you need.

It makes sense.

Charlie That's . . . thank you.

Act One, Scene Three 23

And thank you for apologising.

Sam　I was stressed. I was probably taking it out on you. Like you said.

Deadlines and. Stuff.

Charlie　Yeah, I get it. It's okay. You work too hard.

Pause.

I . . .

Sam　What?

Charlie　Never mind.

Sam　No, what is it?

Charlie　I just want to be really clear. You know I can't . . . you know, chip in?

Or anything. Round here.

Sam　Oh, right, I hadn't –

Charlie　Just to keep things clear. I feel like I should be offering, and I'd love to, but . . . well, I'm barely managing the rent and the bills in my own place and –

Sam　Right, of course.

Charlie　– and you know that I don't have the same . . .

Sam　Yes.

Charlie　Income. As you. Right now.

Sam　Absolutely.

Charlie　And I can't ask my Dad again, it's just not fair on him.

Sam　I . . . No, yeah . . . That's fine.

Pause.

Charlie　Sam.

Sam Yeah?

Charlie You are amazing and I love you. Now, please get some rest.

Sam Okay.

We should get you a key cut –

Sam's *phone starts ringing from another room.*

Oh, is that . . . Shit . . . Errr –

Charlie Stay!

Sam – Where did I leave my phone?

Charlie Stay right there. Don't move.

Charlie *exits to the bedroom.*

Sam (*calling through to* **Charlie**) Who is it?

The phone stops ringing.

Charlie *returns from the bedroom,* **Sam**'s *phone nowhere to be seen.*

Sam Charlie. Who was it?

Charlie It doesn't matter. Now. You need to relax.

Sam Who was it?

Pause.

Charlie.

Charlie She only upsets you.

Sam You need to stop doing that.

Charlie You need to get some rest.

Sam It's not your decision who I –

Charlie You have to admit that this time I'm justified.

Sam I – No. Maybe, but . . .

Charlie Sssh. Relax. Lie back.

Sam . . . Okay . . .

Charlie Chill. I'm calling in sick tomorrow.

Sam You don't have to.

Charlie To keep an eye on you. I want to.

Sam I'll be alright in the morning.

Charlie I don't care. I'm worried about you.

Sam Okay . . . if you're sure you won't get in –

Charlie I'll be your servant for the day. I'll wait on you hand and foot.

Sam Okay.

Charlie And I won't let you out of my sight.

Scene Four

Sam's apartment. Evening.

An empty stage. The sound of keys in the front door and **Sam** *enters, followed closely by* **Charlie**. *They shed coats, bags etc as they speak.*

Sam   Well, it was –

Charlie   Mortifying, Sam. It was mortifying.

Sam   No.

Charlie   Humiliating.

Sam   No. No, look, you're being –

Charlie   *'I'm* being'? 'I'm being' what exactly?

Pause.

Sam   Infantile.

Charlie   Infantile?

Sam   Infantile.

Charlie   Infantile!

Sam   Yes.

Charlie   Fucking hell.

Pause.

Why can't you just say – say – 'you're being a big baby, Charlie?'

Sam   What do you mean?

Charlie   You're always trying to make me feel small. Talking down to me –

Sam   I'm not.

Charlie   – with your big words.

Sam I'm sorry, it's just – it's what came out, I didn't mean to –

Charlie You think you're better than me.

Sam I don't.

Charlie You want me to feel stupid.

Sam I don't think you're stupid, Charlie. I don't think that at all.

Charlie You were embarrassed to be with me. Tonight. I embarrass you.

Sam No.

Charlie They thought they were better than me.

Sam I don't think so.

Charlie I don't like your family, Sam.

Pause.

I'm sorry, but I don't. They're stuck up.

Pause.

You don't like them either.

Sam I do like them.

Pause.

I love them.

Charlie That's not the same thing.

You can love someone and you can not like them.

Sam Yes. Yes, I know . . . You can love someone and despise them, I'm not disputing that. You can really fucking hate the people you love sometimes.

Charlie I didn't ask for the thesis, Sam.

Sam Sorry?

Charlie You're doing it again. You drank too much.

Sam You drank more than I did.

Charlie I can handle it.

Sam And I do like them. I do! I am well aware that you can love someone and not like them, but I love them *and* I like them and – and I would really love it if you liked them too.

Charlie Well, they don't bring out a very nice side of you.

Sam That's . . . Oh. Ouch.

Charlie Also, this is how you feel when it suits you. When it's convenient and fun.

When it's dinner and drinks and they're ooh-ing and aah-ing over your latest list of achievements. But when I'm holding you up at four in the morning and you're choking on your vomit and crying and whining about your – what is it – your 'internalised trauma'. Again. Then it's a different story, isn't it?

Sam I think it's you that's not being very nice, Charlie.

Charlie Well, I think it's you that's being 'infan-ta-whatever-the-fuck'.

Pause.

Sam This can't all be about the bill, can it? Surely.

Charlie It was humiliating.

Sam It doesn't matter. No one cared.

Charlie They did. The way your cousin looked at me.

Sam Morgan is lovely. Morgan wouldn't think anything about – and Morgan also spent years sofa surfing and gigging and so, you know . . . understands that sometimes . . . when . . . I don't know where you've gotten this idea that my family are all . . . they're not materialistic . . . money doesn't . . .

Charlie It's ignorant, Sam. That's what it is.

Sam What's ignorant?

Charlie Assuming. Assuming that everyone can do that. Spending the evening ordering whatever you want – starters, sides, another bottle of wine, a round of after dinner fucking cocktails – and then saying that. 'Oh, we'll be splitting this between the six of us.' Just casually, like it's nothing, like it's obvious. Without asking anyone.

Sam It wasn't done with malice.

Charlie Do you know how it felt watching that card machine work its way round the table? Feeling everyone listening in when it got to our end?

Sam They weren't listening in.

Charlie *Everyone* heard you say it. 'The two of us on my card.' Everyone heard.

Sam But no one minded. No one minded at all.

Charlie It was humiliating.

Sam It's perfectly normal for a couple to pay on the same card! You could have gotten the last one, I could have owed you money for something –

Charlie But I hadn't. And you didn't.

Sam They didn't know that.

Charlie They did. It was humiliating.

Sam You're making a fuss over nothing.

Charlie It was a trap.

Sam What?

Charlie And it *was* intentional.

Sam I . . .

Charlie And it *was* malicious.

Sam . . .

Charlie They wanted to show me that I don't fit in with them.

Sam . . .

Charlie That I don't fit with you.

Sam Charlie, that's ridiculous! We're not the fucking Rockefeller's –

Charlie I know.

Sam We're not – we're – I just have a normal family who don't –

Charlie Normal?

Sam I meant in terms of . . . financially speaking . . .

Look, they don't always go all out like that. It was an occasion.

Charlie It's not actually about the money, Sam. It's . . .

You just don't understand, I guess.

Sam I guess not.

Charlie You just can't see them the way I can.

Sam No.

Charlie You've got this massive blind spot with your whole family.

Sam Maybe.

Charlie There's just so much history there. Damage.

Sam Yeah.

Charlie And don't forget that this was an exception.

Sam . . . to?

Charlie You having a nice time with them tonight was an exception.

Act One, Scene Four   31

Sam Right.

Charlie And you know what they say . . .

Sam . . . ?

Charlie Exception proves the rule.

Sam They do say that.

Charlie Yeah.

Sam Yeah . . .

Charlie I just want to protect you, Sam.

Sam Protect me?

Charlie Yeah. You're so perfect and fragile and brilliant and I wish I could just keep everything with the power to hurt you, just . . . . . . you know . . . just . . . keep it over there. Away from you. Yeah?

Sam Charlie. That's sweet, but –

Charlie You can be a bit naive sometimes, Sam. Which is funny because you're so clever, but you haven't got . . . real . . . smarts, you know? People smarts.

Common sense.

Sam I guess.

Charlie But I do.

Sam Yeah.

Charlie Come here.

Charlie *opens arms wide and* **Sam** *steps into the embrace.*

Charlie Let's not fight.

Sam You're the one that was sulking all the way home.

Charlie I know, I know, you're right. I'm sorry. But you can see why now, yeah?

Sam I guess.

Charlie I was being a big baby, you were right.

Sam Yeah.

Charlie I'll make it up to you tomorrow.

Sam Oh yeah?

Charlie Yeah. I love you.

Sam I love you too.

Scene Five

Sam's apartment. Early evening.

Sam *sits, reading a book. Some time passes.*

We hear keys in the door offstage, **Charlie** *enters, soaked from the rain.*

Charlie Evening.

Sam *reads.*

Charlie Hello.

Sam *maintains a fixed gaze on the page.*

Sam Hi.

Charlie It's pissing rain outside.

Sam Oh yeah?

Charlie Yeah, it's turned into a shite day. It was a nightmare getting home, two buses went by completely full. Honestly, the buses here seriously need to sort their shit out, don't they? The app wasn't even showing the right times, *again*, I thought I was going to have to walk home in this. One showed up eventually, thank fuck, but even then the driver nearly didn't stop. It's bullshit, isn't it?

Total utter bullshit. Isn't it? . . . Hello?

Sam Right, yeah. Bullshit.

Charlie What did you do today?

Sam Hmm?

Charlie What have you done with the day?

Sam Oh, not much. I just – I had some research to do for the, err, for the . . .

Charlie Yeah?

Sam The paper I'm writing.

Charlie Right.

Pause.

Good book?

Sam Not really.

Sam *puts the book down.*

Charlie Have you had dinner?

Sam Not yet.

Charlie What are you making?

Sam I haven't thought about it.

Charlie Well, did you do a shop yet? Because I'm famished. I'll eat you in a minute, if you're not careful!

Pause.

That was a joke.

Sam . . . what was?

Charlie 'I'll eat . . .' I – ah, fuck's sake. Never mind then. I was just trying to make you laugh.

Sam Oh, right. Sorry. I didn't realise. It's not really a joke.

Charlie Well, it's not like I'm literally going to eat you is it? But fine, fine – maybe it's not a 'joke' joke, but I was messing around, you know. Just trying to be silly, make you laugh.

Sam Sorry.

. . . Ha. Ha.

Charlie Well you're in a shit mood.

Sam Sorry.

Charlie So did you get any food in?

Sam No.

Charlie So you've just been sitting around at home all day?

Act One, Scene Five   35

Sam I've been working at home all day, yeah. Researching. For a paper. For work.

Charlie Alright, alright, sorry – Jesus.

Pause.

So, what do you want to do?

Sam What do you mean?

Charlie For food. What do you want to eat?

Sam I don't know. I haven't thought about it.

Charlie Well, do you want to think about it now?

Sam Fine.

Charlie Christ, you're no craic tonight. Work was shit, you know – not that you've asked – then I had to get home in *this* and I spend the whole day looking forward to coming back and seeing you and now you'll hardly say two words to me. That's just great.

Sam I'm sorry.

Charlie That's okay, that's okay.

Charlie's *tone shifts.*

So, what can we do to cheer you up, eh?

Sam I don't know.

Charlie *is physically closer to* **Sam** *now . . . maybe they try a touch, maybe a kiss.*

Sam *flinches away and re-establishes physical distance. Tense.*

There is a non-verbal dialogue to be found between them here.

The language of breath and bodies in space. Eye contact or no eye contact?

This takes as long as it takes.

Sam Get a Deliveroo if you want.

Charlie Okay. Okay, yeah. That'd be nice. Bit of takeaway, maybe stick something on Netflix. I don't get paid till Thursday though, so I'll put it on your card, yeah?

Sam No, don't. I don't want anything.

Charlie What? Oh, for fuck's sake.

Sam Well, I don't think it's fair that I keep paying for your shit.

Charlie Well, I don't think it's fair that you said you'd do a shop today and didn't.

Sam Right. A shop – which I would also have paid for, and you would have eaten most of.

Charlie Christ alright, I guess we're not eating then. I don't know why you're being such a cunt all of a sudden. You do realise it's completely crazy that you get in these moods out of nowhere and you expect me just to take it? I'm knackered. I've been at work all day.

Sam Are we ever going to talk about it?

Charlie Talk about what?

Sam It. The other night. It.

Charlie What's 'it'?

Sam I think we need to talk about it. I need us to talk about it.

Charlie *laughs*.

Charlie Are you tapped?

Sam Don't do that.

Charlie Do what?

Sam I've told you I hate it when you call me that.

Charlie Tapped?

Sam Tapped. Nuts. Crazy. Psycho. Any descriptor for a mentally ill person, basically.

Charlie Ah, Jesus. You know I don't mean it like that. It's a turn of phrase.

Sam It's not a turn of phrase.

Charlie It is, it's just something people say.

Sam Not to a person who – and it isn't. I don't know anyone else who calls anyone else that and it – I find it hurtful, you always telling me I can't trust myself.

Charlie What? That's a jump, Sam. That's totally out of the blue. I've never done that.

Sam You have. That I'm crazy and psycho and irrational and moody and I can't trust my own judgement because I'm mentally ill because of my 'fucked up childhood', like yours was so perfect, and –

Charlie Woah, woah, woah. Chill out. Chill. Seriously, I've never said any of that.

Sam No, not literally, not exactly, but you imply it. You make me feel like –

Charlie That's in your head, Sam.

Sam Like that! Stop it!

Charlie Oh my –

Sam This isn't the point anyway. It's. I want to talk about –

Charlie Yes. Right, 'it'. Sorry – sorry! Go on then, this mysterious 'it' –

Sam Don't do that. You know exactly what I'm talking about.

Charlie Okay great . . . It.

It, it, it, it it . . . hmm . . .

Sam The other night.

Pause.

I'd strained my neck again – and you said . . . you offered to . . . and then . . .

Pause.

I really need us to talk about it.

Charlie   . . .

The – okay . . .

Sam I said no.

Long pause.

Charlie Right.

That.

Yeah.

Long pause.

Sam I didn't want –

Charlie I know.

Sam And you – you just – anyway.

Charlie Yeah.

Sam And then you just went to sleep.

Long pause.

And I haven't been able to stop thinking about it.

Act One, Scene Six   39

Scene Six

Sam's apartment. Night.

Charlie *enters from the bedroom in a state of urgency – but suddenly lacks direction. Doesn't know whether to sit or stand. Frantic. Floundering. Maybe sits. Maybe not.*

Eventually **Sam** *enters from the bedroom.*

Charlie I'm sorry, Sam, I'm so sorry.

Sam.

I'm.

I'm so, so sorry, Sam.

Sam Yeah, it's – I know.

Charlie I'm so –

Sam I know.

Charlie So sorry.

Sam I know.

Charlie I'm a piece of shit.

Sam Don't.

Charlie I'm a fucking piece of shit and you're amazing.

Sam Please don't.

Charlie You're amazing and I love you so much.

Sam Charlie.

Charlie Do you still love me, Sam?

Pause.

I know. I know, I'm sorry. Sorry. Look, I'm really trying here. I'm really – I'm trying so hard because I – look, I want to be better for you, Sam. I do.

But it's like everything I do is wrong. Everything I do annoys you, Sam. Sam?

Sam Charlie, I can't have this fight again. We need to get ready. We need to go.

Beat.

Charlie Do we have to go?

Sam I. Well. Yes. I think we do have to.

Charlie We don't have to. We have to stay here and sort this out. I love you.

Sam There's nothing to sort out. It was – we're bickering. I wanted some space for a minute, that's all. And I do have to actually. I need to go tonight. It's for my – it's for work. I have to.

Charlie It's a party.

Sam No, it's – yes, I know. It's an. Event. It's a work-related event.

Charlie It's not compulsory.

Sam People will notice if I don't go.

Charlie Do you want to go?

Sam I – I don't know. Yes. Well, right now not particularly, no. But yes, I do.

Apart from anything else it's a networking opportunity.

Charlie A networking opportunity?

Sam Yes.

Pause.

Charlie God. You can be so cold sometimes.

Sam Cold?

Charlie I just didn't realise how little our relationship meant to you.

Pause.

Please don't go.

Pause.

Look, I love how ambitious you are, Sam. You know that. I love how clever and brilliant you are. I love that you're so good at what you do. I love that about you. But you really need to learn to switch it off. If you can't prioritise us over your work every now and then, when it matters, then you're going to kill this. What we have. I hope you realise that. I really need you here tonight. I want to work on this. On us. I know that what we have is so, so special. I know that. You know that too, yeah?

Sam *nods.*

Charlie And I want to fix this. I really want to make this better. Don't you?

Sam *nods.*

Charlie Yeah. Yeah. Good.

Long pause.

Sam They're also my friends.

Charlie What?

Pause.

Who?

Sam I have a lot of friends going tonight. Friends I haven't really seen much of recently. In quite a long time actually. I've been looking forward to it.

Charlie They're not your friends.

Sam Yes, they are.

Charlie Who? Frankie?

Sam Charlie!

Charlie I know, I know. Fuck's sake. Sorry.

But seriously though, who? Who's going tonight that is actually a friend of yours? A real friend. They're – they're all. None of them like me.

Sam It's not that they don't like you, they just . . . they worry . . . since . . .

Charlie Oh, right. That.

Pause.

Alex is a gossip.

Sam Alex was concerned.

Charlie You said you didn't want anyone to know.

Sam Charlie.

Charlie And then you tell someone who *you know* will tell everyone. *Everyone.*

It was our private business.

Sam I'm sorry.

Charlie And now all your friends hate me.

Sam They don't hate you.

Charlie Do you hate me?

Sam . . . I . . .

Charlie Because this is what we're really fighting about isn't it?

Sam Honestly, Charlie . . . I –

Charlie This is what it's all really about, isn't it?

Sam What do you mean?

Charlie We're not just bickering.

Pause.

Is that why you told Alex? Because you hate me.

Sam No.

Charlie You want them to hate me. You want everyone to hate me.

Sam No, no. I – I don't . . . know.

Charlie You're the one that said no one would understand.

Sam I know.

Charlie You forgave me. You said you'd forgiven me. You said we'd forget it.

Sam I know, I'm sorry. I did. I thought I had, I thought I could. But I didn't.

Charlie You said we'd keep it between us.

Sam I know, I'm sorry. I was drunk. It slipped out.

Charlie And now everyone knows our personal business.

Sam I'm –

Charlie And you punish me every fucking day, Sam.

Sam I don't mean to.

Charlie You say we've moved on, but you just drag it back up – you want –

Sam It's confusing.

Charlie You know what, fuck you, Sam.

Beat.

Fuck you. You're a fucking liar. You're a manipulative –

You're. You fucking – fuck sake –

Fuck!

Sam Please stop –

Charlie How would you like it if everyone knew the worst thing you had ever done, Sam? Yeah? Would you like to be judged by your lowest moment? Would you? Your biggest mistake? Do you want me to hate myself, Sam?

Sam No –

Charlie Well I do, I do, I fucking hate myself. I've been trying to keep it together for you, Sam. I've been trying to make it all better, for you. But actually – inside – I actually want to fucking kill myself. Maybe that's what you want. Is it? Is that what you want to hear, Sam? That I want to die?

Sam Charlie –

Charlie I never get to undo it, Sam. I never get to go back in time and not do that. I have to live with that every single fucking day. I have to look in the mirror and know that I hurt you. Know that I love you so much and I hurt you. If anyone else hurt you like that I'd slaughter them, I'd end them, I'd – but I did that. Do you know how that feels, Sam? Do you? Can you imagine how that feels? I'm nothing. I'm . . . I did that and I can't take it back. I can't.

And I'm a . . .

And I'm a fucking . . .

Sam You don't have to say it.

Charlie I should be punished. I should. No wonder you hate me.

Suddenly **Charlie** *begins to hit themself over and over.*

Sam Charlie! Stop it, stop it, stop it, stop it, stop it.

Sam *says as many 'stop it's as are necessary until they can make* **Charlie** *stop.*

Sam Sssh. Shush, Charlie. It's okay, ssh. It's. I know, I know.

Charlie I'm a. For the rest of my life.

Sam It's okay, ssh. Sssh.

Sam *holds and soothes* **Charlie**.

Sam It doesn't matter. I know it was a mistake. And I know you know that.

It was a mistake. It was just a mistake.

Charlie I'm. I'm so . . .

. . .

Sam It doesn't . . . It doesn't define you. That one thing.

Pause.

It doesn't. You're so much more than that. People make mistakes. You're a human being. You're . . .

Pause.

I'm sorry I told Alex. And I'm sorry Alex told other people. You're right, they don't understand and . . . and we're working on it. It'll be okay. I'm sorry that I'm still . . . I'm still finding it so hard to . . . to move past it and I'm sorry . . .

Pause.

Charlie That's okay.

Sam I'm trying.

Charlie I know.

Sam And I will.

Charlie Yeah.

Sam We'll be okay.

Charlie Yeah.

Sam We won't go tonight.

Charlie Okay.

Sam We'll stay right here.

Charlie Thank you.

Sam I love you.

Charlie Thank you.

Sam I love you so much.

Charlie I love you too.

Scene Seven

Sam's apartment. Day.

Sam *and* **Charlie** *are silent. Far apart from one another. Not looking at each other.*

Sam *has a visible injury, a few days old. Perhaps a black eye, bruising or scratch marks.*

Silence.

Sam　You . . .

Pause.

Charlie　Yes.

Silence.

Sam　You . . .

Pause.

Charlie　I know.

Silence.

Sam　You . . . Charlie, you . . .

Charlie　Yes.

Sam　You hurt me.

Charlie　I know.

Pause.

I'm sorry.

Sam　Yes.

Charlie　I am – I really am so, so sorry, Sam.

Sam　I know.

Pause.

Charlie.

Charlie Yes?

Pause.

Sam I . . . There has to be a line.

Charlie What do you mean?

Sam There has to be. There has to be a line somewhere.

Charlie I didn't mean it.

Sam I cannot become this, Charlie. I refuse.

I have to . . . There has to be a limit.

Charlie I love you so much, Sam.

Sam There has to be a line, somewhere, there has to be a limit and . . . and this. Charlie. This has to be it.

Charlie I really –

Sam This has to be that line, Charlie. We've crossed it.

Charlie I really do – I adore you. I'm so sorry.

Sam It's been crossed now. So. So this is the. This is the end. Now. It has to be.

Long pause.

Charlie.

Silence.

Charlie Thank you for agreeing to have this talk with me, Sam.

Sam Did you hear what I just said to you?

Charlie I was losing my mind when you weren't talking to me.

Sam I know that you're intentionally averting this / conversa –

Charlie / I mean . . . *blocking* me. A bit. Extreme. Cruel really. Wasn't it?

Well, you made your point anyway. I've learnt my lesson.

Sam No. No lesson, Charlie. This relationship – it's over.

Charlie It's not over, Sam.

Sam It is.

Charlie It's not.

Sam What do you mean, it's not? Charlie, you sound . . .

Charlie Crazy? I know. I sound crazy. But I'm not. I know I'm not. Do you know why?

Sam What are you trying to . . .

Charlie Do you know why? Sam? Why, I'm not crazy? Why, I know it's not over?

Pause.

Sam Why?

Charlie Because you let me in that door, there. Because you still love me.

Sam Charlie.

Charlie I'm right.

Sam Charlie.

Charlie Tell me I'm wrong.

Sam You're wrong.

Charlie I'm not wrong. Because you said you never wanted to see me again and you said that was it. You said we were finished. You said you were scared of me.

And I get that I scared you, but you're not scared *of* me, Sam, because you let me inside here. You let me in. And that's how I know we're not done.

Sam I shouldn't have.

Charlie I have missed you so much this week. It's made me realise what losing you would be like and I can't lose you, Sam. I swear, I'll never hurt you again.

Sam. Never.

Pause.

I'll spend the rest of my life making it up to you, Sam. Forever, Sam.

Sam I need you to accept that we're breaking up, Charlie.

Charlie But that's not what you want.

Sam It is what I want.

Charlie No, it's what you think you're supposed to want.

Sam What?

Charlie Because I fucked up. I've fucked up a lot. I know that Sam. But I'm changing.

Sam You can't just say that every time that you –

Charlie Who have you told?

Sam What do you mean?

Charlie What I did – I messed up, I really messed up – and – who have you told?

Someone's telling you what to – you've got opinions in your head, I can tell.

Who have you told?

Pause.

Sam No one.

Charlie Your mum?

Sam We haven't been speaking.

Charlie Your friends?

Sam No, Charlie. They already think I'm such a fucking idiot for staying with you after the last thing. That I – I couldn't . . . No, I didn't tell them.

Charlie You really haven't told anyone?

Sam No. I haven't spoken to anyone. I haven't even been leaving the house.

Charlie God. Oh, Sam. Sammy. I'm so sorry.

Silence.

Do you remember that Airbnb in Scotland? That weekend?

Pause.

Do you remember?

Sam Of course I remember.

Charlie When I got us that Airbnb in Scotland. It was your birthday. Remember?

Sam Yes. I remember.

Charlie The first birthday we spent together. We hadn't been dating that long.

Sam No.

Charlie And I surprised you. And I was so worried that I'd have fucked it up – booked it wrong, somehow, or – but it was beautiful.

Pause.

Sam It was nice. Yeah.

Charlie Nice? That was the happiest I've ever been in my entire life, Sam.

Pause.

That weekend was the happiest I've ever been.

Sam Charlie.

Charlie In our tiny home in the Scottish hills.

Sam I think you should go.

Charlie Our little hill-side cabin.

Pause.

That view. And those sunsets. The sun setting over the lake.

The sky was all pink and blue.

Do you remember?

Pause.

And the birds in the morning.

And no one around. Just us and the birds. And the lake. Loch?

Ha! You kept correcting me, remember? 'They call it a loch, Charlie.'

You kept telling me. And I kept forgetting. I'd forgotten that.

Just us and the birds and the loch.

And we were so in love. We had so much love we didn't need anything else.

Sam You can't do this, Charlie. It's not fair.

Charlie You said that weekend that we would have to remember how much we loved each other, whenever things got hard. You said that. You said that you'd never loved anyone like you love me and that that meant that we could work through anything. You said that couples only break up because most people aren't willing to do the work, to really work hard at things together. They give up. That as long as we were willing to work on things, and remembered how much we loved each other, and never gave up, that we would be fine. You said that. Well, I am willing to work on this, Sam. And I won't give up.

Are you saying you want to give / up, Sam?

Sam / Things are different now, / Charlie.

Charlie / They're not different, Sam! I still love you that much. And if I still love you and you still love me then that is literally all that matters. We can get through anything. Like you said. Like you said as we sat on the edge of that fucking lake, Sam, watching that perfect fucking sunset from our perfect fucking cabin as you held me in your perfect fucking arms, Sam, please –

Sam This isn't fair.

Charlie Please, Sam. We'll work on this.

Sam You can't just. You can't. You can't just not *accept* that we are breaking up, Charlie, you can't –

Charlie You've taught me a lesson, Sam. It'll be different.

Sam No. You can't do this. You can't just say 'remember the good times' and guilt trip me into . . .

Pause.

If someone says, 'we're done, I'm leaving you', you can't just say 'no, actually, that doesn't work for me'.

Pause.

Charlie If I thought that's what you actually wanted, Sam, I'd be gone in a second.

Yes, it'd fucking hurt. It would break my heart. Sam. You would break my heart. But I would go, I would. I'd do it because I only want what's best for you. I would do it for you, Sam. But I know that that's not what you want.

Long pause.

Come here.

Sam No.

Charlie Please, Sam. Come over here. Just for a second.

Pause.

. . . Please.

Sam   . . . No.

Charlie   . . . Sam . . .

Same   . . . No . . .

Charlie *opens arms wide.* **Sam** *shakes their head 'No'.*

But eventually . . .

. . . **Sam** *reluctantly, hesitantly, gradually makes their way into* **Charlie**'s *arms.*

They embrace: tense and awkward at first, uncertain, but gradually softening, giving in to it. Then squeezing, like they're holding on for dear life.

Charlie   Thank you.

Pause.

Thank you. Thank you, Sammy, I just needed to hold you.

Thank you. Thank you. Thank you. Thank you.

I love you. I love you so much, I don't know what I would do without you.

They hold each other.

Silence.

Sammy?

Sam   Mmhmm.

Charlie   What are you thinking?

Pause.

Sam   I don't know.

Charlie   You can tell me.

Sam   I know. I . . . I know I can. But. I can't . . . I don't think I'm thinking anything.

Charlie No?

Sam No.

Charlie Okay.

Pause.

Are we going to be okay?

Pause.

Sam I don't know.

Charlie Okay.

They hold each other. They breathe together, **Charlie** *stroking* **Sam** *gently.*

Charlie Sam.

Sam.

Sammy.

Sam?

Sam Mmhmm.

Charlie Sam.

Sam Yeah, Charlie. I said yeah.

Charlie Do you still love me?

Pause.

Sam Yes.

Charlie Yeah. You sure?

Sam Yes, Charlie.

Charlie Good.

Interval.

Act Two

Notes on **Act Two** *. . .*

We now play the scenes again in reverse order.

Each scene should be played by a different pair of actors than the pair we've seen playing that scene in **Act One**. *If we do see the same two actors playing the same scene with each other, they will each be playing the opposite role. An actor might play the same scene in both acts, but if they do, then either the actor they are playing the scene with, the character they are playing in the scene, or both, will change.*

In **Act Two** *the actors should all swap roles, once or more than once.*

The actors who played **Sam** *in* **Act One** *should begin this act playing* **Charlie**, *and the actors who played* **Charlie** *in* **Act One** *should begin this act playing* **Sam**.

As an example, here is how casting for the original production played out in Act Two . . .

Act Two

Scene 1: Sam – Curtis-Lee/Eavan   Charlie – Jeanne/Matthew
Scene 2: Sam – Eavan   Charlie – Jeanne
Scene 3: Sam – Eavan   Charlie – Matthew
Scene 4: Sam – Curtis-Lee   Charlie – Matthew
Scene 5: Sam – Curtis-Lee/Eavan   Charlie – Jeanne/Matthew
Scene 6: Sam – Jeanne   Charlie – Matthew/Eavan
Scene 7: Sam – Curtis-Lee   Charlie – Eavan
Epilogue: Charlie – Eavan, Other Charlie – Jeanne, Sam – Curtis-Lee, Other Sam – Matthew

Throughout **Act Two** *you might also play with having non-speaking actors present as their character, unseen by the characters playing the scene. You might play with unison, repetition of lines (or whole scenes), mirroring moments, experimental scene changes, or any other abstractions. Essentially,* **Act Two** *is free game. As long as all of the text is spoken (at least once) it can be distorted and* *played with in whatever ways you wish. You may even choose to disregard the stage directions and make different choices in this act, wherever you feel appropriate.*

I have found that it is helpful to consider that the stakes must continue to rise, despite us going backwards in chronology. Do not ignore what has come before. Yes, the scenes are going back in time, but what if our characters are not? What if they are merely circling? Replaying their memories? Trying to make sense of what has come before? Stuck in limbo? Stuck in a nightmare? Slipping through cracks in the multiverse? In short, they need no longer exist in the world of naturalism at all. Injuries and/or actions should now be exaggerated and/or distorted. If the characters ever lied or manipulated well, they should now do so less successfully. Any 'red flags' that were well hidden should now be brought to the fore. Interpret this how you will.

There is also a short epilogue in which all actors should appear on the stage.

Scene One

Sam's apartment. Day.

Sam *and* **Charlie** *are silent. Far apart from one another. Not looking at each other.*

Sam *has a visible injury, a few days old. Perhaps a huge black eye, extensive bruising, scratch marks or an arm in a sling.*

Silence.

Sam You . . .

Pause.

Charlie Yes.

Silence.

Sam You . . .

Pause.

Charlie I know.

Silence.

Sam You . . . Charlie, you . . .

Charlie Yes.

Sam You hurt me.

Charlie I know.

Pause.

I'm sorry.

Sam Yes.

Charlie I am – I really am so, so sorry, Sam.

Sam I know.

Pause.

Charlie.

Charlie Yes?

Pause.

Sam I . . . There has to be a line.

Charlie What do you mean?

Sam There has to be. There has to be a line somewhere.

Charlie I didn't mean it.

Sam I cannot become this, Charlie. I refuse.

I have to . . . There has to be a limit.

Charlie I love you so much, Sam.

Sam There has to be a line, somewhere, there has to be a limit and . . . and this. Charlie. This has to be it.

Charlie I really –

Sam This has to be that line, Charlie. We've crossed it.

Charlie I really do – I adore you. I'm so sorry.

Sam It's been crossed now. So. So this is the. This is the end. Now. It has to be.

Long pause.

Charlie.

Silence.

Charlie Thank you for agreeing to have this talk with me, Sam.

Sam Did you hear what I just said to you?

Charlie I was losing my mind when you weren't talking to me.

Sam I know that you're intentionally averting this /
conversa –

Charlie / I mean . . . *blocking* me. A bit. Extreme. Cruel really. Wasn't it?

Well, you made your point anyway. I've learnt my lesson.

Sam No. No lesson, Charlie. This relationship – it's over.

Charlie It's not over, Sam.

Sam It is.

Charlie It's not.

Sam What do you mean, it's not? Charlie, you sound . . .

Charlie Crazy? I know. I sound crazy. But I'm not. I know I'm not. Do you know why?

Sam What are you trying to . . .

Charlie Do you know why? Sam? Why, I'm not crazy? Why, I know it's not over?

Pause.

Sam Why?

Charlie Because you let me in that door, there. Because you still love me.

Sam Charlie.

Charlie I'm right.

Sam Charlie.

Charlie Tell me I'm wrong.

Sam You're wrong.

Charlie I'm not wrong. Because you said you never wanted to see me again and you said that was it. You said we were finished. You said you were scared of me.

And I get that I scared you, but you're not scared *of* me, Sam, because you let me inside here. You let me in. And that's how I know we're not done.

Sam I shouldn't have.

Charlie I have missed you so much this week. It's made me realise what losing you would be like and I can't lose you, Sam. I swear, I'll never hurt you again, Sam. Never.

Pause.

I'll spend the rest of my life making it up to you, Sam. Forever, Sam.

Sam I need you to accept that we're breaking up, Charlie.

Charlie But that's not what you want.

Sam It is what I want.

Charlie No, it's what you think you're supposed to want.

Sam What?

Charlie Because I fucked up. I've fucked up a lot. I know that Sam. But I'm changing.

Sam You can't just say that every time that you –

Charlie Who have you told?

Sam What do you mean?

Charlie What I did – I messed up, I really messed up – and – who have you told?

Someone's telling you what to – you've got opinions in your head, I can tell.

Who have you told?

Pause.

Sam No one.

Charlie Your mum?

Sam We haven't been speaking.

Charlie Your friends?

Sam No, Charlie. They already think I'm such a fucking idiot for staying with you after the last thing. That I – I couldn't . . . No, I didn't tell them.

Charlie You really haven't told anyone?

Sam No. I haven't spoken to anyone. I haven't even been leaving the house.

Charlie God. Oh, Sam. Sammy. I'm so sorry.

Silence.

Do you remember that Airbnb in Scotland? That weekend?

Pause.

Do you remember?

Sam Of course I remember.

Charlie When I got us that Airbnb in Scotland. It was your birthday. Remember

Sam Yes. I remember.

Charlie The first birthday we spent together. We hadn't been dating that long.

Sam No.

Charlie And I surprised you. And I was so worried that I'd have fucked it up – booked it wrong, somehow, or – but it was beautiful.

Pause.

Sam It was nice. Yeah.

Charlie Nice? That was the happiest I've ever been in my entire life, Sam.

Pause.

That weekend was the happiest I've ever been.

Sam Charlie.

Charlie In our tiny home in the Scottish hills.

Sam I think you should go.

Charlie Our little hill-side cabin.

Pause.

That view. And those sunsets. The sun setting over the lake.

The sky was all pink and blue.

Do you remember?

Pause.

And the birds in the morning.

And no one around. Just us and the birds. And the lake. Loch?

Ha! You kept correcting me, remember? 'They call it a loch, Charlie.'

You kept telling me. And I kept forgetting. I'd forgotten that.

Just us and the birds and the loch.

And we were so in love. We had so much love we didn't need anything else.

Sam You can't do this, Charlie. It's not fair.

Charlie You said that weekend that we would have to remember how much we loved each other, whenever things got hard. You said that. You said that you'd never loved anyone like you love me and that that meant that we could work through anything. You said that couples only break up because most people aren't willing to do the work, to really work hard at things together. They give up. That as long as we were willing to work on things, and remembered how much we loved each other, and never gave up, that we would be fine. You said that. Well, I am willing to work on this, Sam. And I won't give up.

Are you saying you want to give / up, Sam?

Sam / Things are different now, / Charlie.

Charlie / They're not different, Sam! I still love you that much. And if I still love you and you still love me then that is literally all that matters. We can get through anything. Like you said. Like you said as we sat on the edge of that fucking lake, Sam, watching that perfect fucking sunset from our perfect fucking cabin as you held me in your perfect fucking arms, Sam, please –

Sam This isn't fair.

Charlie Please, Sam. We'll work on this.

Sam You can't just. You can't. You can't just not *accept* that we are breaking up, Charlie, you can't –

Charlie You've taught me a lesson, Sam. It'll be different.

Sam No. You can't do this. You can't just say 'remember the good times' and guilt trip me into . . .

Pause.

If someone says, 'we're done, I'm leaving you', you can't just say 'no, actually, that doesn't work for me'.

Pause.

Charlie If I thought that's what you actually wanted, Sam, I'd be gone in a second.

Yes, it'd fucking hurt. It would break my heart. Sam. You would break my heart. But I would go, I would. I'd do it because I only want what's best for you. I would do it for you, Sam. But I know that that's not what you want.

Long pause.

Come here.

Sam No.

Charlie Please, Sam. Come over here. Just for a second.

Pause.

. . . Please.

Sam . . . No.

Charlie . . . Sam . . .

Same . . . No . . .

Charlie *opens arms wide.* **Sam** *shakes their head 'No'.*

But eventually . . .

. . . **Sam** *reluctantly, hesitantly, gradually makes their way into* **Charlie**'s *arms.*

They embrace: tense and awkward at first, uncertain, but gradually softening, giving in to it. Then squeezing, like they're holding on for dear life.

Charlie Thank you.

Pause.

Thank you. Thank you, Sammy, I just needed to hold you.

Thank you. Thank you. Thank you. Thank you.

I love you. I love you so much, I don't know what I would do without you.

They hold each other.

Silence.

Sammy?

Sam Mmhmm.

Charlie What are you thinking?

Pause.

Sam I don't know.

Charlie You can tell me.

Sam I know. I . . . I know I can. But. I can't . . . I don't think I'm thinking anything.

Charlie No?

Sam No.

Charlie Okay.

Pause.

Are we going to be okay?

Pause.

Sam I don't know.

Charlie Okay.

They hold each other. They breathe together, **Charlie** *stroking* **Sam** *gently.*

Charlie Sam.

Sam.

Sammy.

Sam?

Sam Mmhmm.

Charlie Sam.

Sam Yeah, Charlie. I said yeah.

Charlie Do you still love me?

Pause.

Sam Yes.

Charlie Yeah. You sure?

Sam Yes, Charlie.

Charlie Good.

Scene Two

Sam's apartment. Night.

Charlie *enters from the bedroom in a state of urgency – but suddenly lacks direction. Doesn't know whether to sit or stand. Frantic. Floundering. Maybe sits. Maybe not.*

Eventually **Sam** *enters from the bedroom.*

Charlie I'm sorry, Sam, I'm so sorry.

Sam.

I'm.

I'm so, so sorry, Sam.

Sam Yeah, it's – I know.

Charlie I'm so –

Sam I know.

Charlie So sorry.

Sam I know.

Charlie I'm a piece of shit.

Sam Don't.

Charlie I'm a fucking piece of shit and you're amazing.

Sam Please don't.

Charlie You're amazing and I love you so much.

Sam Charlie.

Charlie Do you still love me, Sam?

Pause.

I know. I know, I'm sorry. Sorry. Look, I'm really trying here. I'm really – I'm trying so hard because I – look, I want to be better for you, Sam. I do.

But it's like everything I do is wrong. Everything I do annoys you, Sam. Sam?

Sam Charlie, I can't have this fight again. We need to get ready. We need to go.

Beat.

Charlie Do we have to go?

Sam I. Well. Yes. I think we do have to.

Charlie We don't have to. We have to stay here and sort this out. I love you.

Sam There's nothing to sort out. It was – we're bickering. I wanted some space for a minute, that's all. And I do have to actually. I need to go tonight. It's for my – it's for work. I have to.

Charlie It's a party.

Sam No, it's – yes, I know. It's an. Event. It's a work-related event.

Charlie It's not compulsory.

Sam People will notice if I don't go.

Charlie Do you want to go?

Sam I – I don't know. Yes. Well, right now not particularly, no. But yes, I do.

Apart from anything else it's a networking opportunity.

Charlie A networking opportunity?

Sam Yes.

Pause.

Charlie God. You can be so cold sometimes.

Sam Cold?

Charlie I just didn't realise how little our relationship meant to you.

Pause.

Please don't go.

Pause.

Look, I love how ambitious you are, Sam. You know that. I love how clever and brilliant you are. I love that you're so good at what you do. I love that about you. But you really need to learn to switch it off. If you can't prioritise us over your work every now and then, when it matters, then you're going to kill this. What we have. I hope you realise that. I really need you here tonight. I want to work on this. On us. I know that what we have is so, so special. I know that. You know that too, yeah?

Sam *nods.*

Charlie And I want to fix this. I really want to make this better. Don't you?

Sam *nods.*

Charlie Yeah. Yeah. Good.

Long pause.

Sam They're also my friends.

Charlie What?

Pause.

Who?

Sam I have a lot of friends going tonight. Friends I haven't really seen much of recently. In quite a long time actually. I've been looking forward to it.

Charlie They're not your friends.

Sam Yes, they are.

Charlie Who? Frankie?

Sam Charlie!

Charlie I know, I know. Fuck's sake. Sorry.

But seriously though, who? Who's going tonight that is actually a friend of yours? A real friend. They're – they're all. None of them like me.

Sam It's not that they don't like you, they just . . . they worry . . . since . . .

Charlie Oh, right. That.

Pause.

Alex is a gossip.

Sam Alex was concerned.

Charlie You said you didn't want anyone to know.

Sam Charlie.

Charlie And then you tell someone who *you know* will tell everyone. *Everyone.*

It was our private business.

Sam I'm sorry.

Charlie And now all your friends hate me.

Sam They don't hate you.

Charlie Do you hate me?

Sam . . . I . . .

Charlie Because this is what we're really fighting about isn't it?

Sam Honestly, Charlie . . . I –

Charlie This is what it's all really about, isn't it?

Sam What do you mean?

Charlie We're not just bickering.

Pause.

Is that why you told Alex? Because you hate me.

Sam No.

Charlie You want them to hate me. You want everyone to hate me.

Sam No, no. I – I don't . . . know.

Charlie You're the one that said no one would understand.

Sam I know.

Charlie You forgave me. You said you'd forgiven me. You said we'd forget it.

Sam I know, I'm sorry. I did. I thought I had, I thought I could. But I didn't.

Charlie You said we'd keep it between us.

Sam I know, I'm sorry. I was drunk. It slipped out.

Charlie And now everyone knows our personal business.

Sam I'm –

Charlie And you punish me every fucking day, Sam.

Sam I don't mean to.

Charlie You say we've moved on, but you just drag it back up – you want –

Sam It's confusing.

Charlie You know what, fuck you, Sam.

Beat.

Fuck you. You're a fucking liar. You're a manipulative –

You're. You fucking – fuck sake –

Fuck!

Sam Please stop –

Charlie How would you like it if everyone knew the worst thing you had ever done, Sam? Yeah? Would you like to be judged by your lowest moment? Would you? Your biggest mistake? Do you want me to hate myself, Sam?

Sam No –

Charlie Well I do, I do, I fucking hate myself. I've been trying to keep it together for you, Sam. I've been trying to make it all better, for you. But actually – inside –

I actually want to fucking kill myself. Maybe that's what you want. Is it? Is that what you want to hear, Sam? That I want to die?

Sam Charlie –

Charlie I never get to undo it, Sam. I never get to go back in time and not do that. I have to live with that every single fucking day. I have to look in the mirror and know that I hurt you. Know that I love you so much and I hurt you. If anyone else hurt you like that I'd slaughter them, I'd end them, I'd – but I did that. Do you know how that feels, Sam? Do you? Can you imagine how that feels? I'm nothing. I'm . . . I did that and I can't take it back. I can't.

And I'm a . . .

And I'm a fucking . . .

Sam You don't have to say it.

Charlie I should be punished. I should. No wonder you hate me.

Suddenly **Charlie** *begins to hit themself over and over.*

Sam Charlie! Stop it, stop it, stop it, stop it, stop it.

Sam *says as many 'stop it's' as are necessary until they can make* **Charlie** *stop.*

Sam Sssh. Shush, Charlie. It's okay, ssh. It's. I know, I know.

Charlie I'm a. For the rest of my life.

Sam It's okay, ssh. Sssh.

Sam *holds and soothes* **Charlie**.

Sam It doesn't matter. I know it was a mistake. And I know you know that.

It was a mistake. It was just a mistake . . .

Charlie I'm. I'm so . . .

. . .

Sam It doesn't . . . It doesn't define you. That one thing.

Pause.

It doesn't. You're so much more than that. People make mistakes. You're a human being. You're . . .

Pause.

I'm sorry I told Alex. And I'm sorry Alex told other people. You're right, they don't understand and . . . and we're working on it. It'll be okay. I'm sorry that I'm still . . . I'm still finding it so hard to . . . to move past it and I'm sorry . . .

Pause.

Charlie That's okay.

Sam I'm trying.

Charlie I know.

Sam And I will.

Charlie Yeah.

Sam We'll be okay.

Charlie Yeah.

Sam We won't go tonight.

Charlie Okay.

Sam We'll stay right here.

Charlie Thank you.

Sam I love you.

Charlie Thank you.

Sam I love you so much.

Charlie I love you too.

Scene Three

Sam's apartment. Early evening.

Sam *sits, reading a book. Some time passes.*

We hear keys in the door offstage, **Charlie** *enters, soaked from the rain.*

Charlie   Evening.

Sam *reads*

Charlie   Hello.

Sam *maintains a fixed gaze on the page.*

Sam   Hi.

Charlie   It's pissing rain outside.

Sam   Oh yeah?

Charlie   Yeah, it's turned into a shite day. It was a nightmare getting home, two buses went by completely full. Honestly, the buses here seriously need to sort their shit out, don't they? The app wasn't even showing the right times, *again*, I thought I was going to have to walk home in this. One showed up eventually, thank fuck, but even then the driver nearly didn't stop. It's bullshit, isn't it?

Total utter bullshit. Isn't it? . . . Hello?

Sam   Right, yeah. Bullshit.

Charlie   What did you do today?

Sam   Hmm?

Charlie   What have you done with the day?

Sam   Oh, not much. I just – I had some research to do for the, err, for the . . .

Charlie   Yeah?

Sam   The paper I'm writing.

Charlie Right.

Pause.

Good book?

Sam Not really.

Sam *puts the book down.*

Charlie Have you had dinner?

Sam Not yet.

Charlie What are you making?

Sam I haven't thought about it.

Charlie Well, did you do a shop yet? Because I'm famished. I'll eat you in a minute, if you're not careful!

Pause.

That was a joke.

Sam . . . what was?

Charlie 'I'll eat . . .' I – ah, fuck's sake. Never mind then. I was just trying to make you laugh.

Sam Oh, right. Sorry. I didn't realise. It's not really a joke.

Charlie Well, it's not like I'm literally going to eat you is it? But fine, fine – maybe it's not a 'joke' joke, but I was messing around, you know. Just trying to be silly, make you laugh.

Sam Sorry.

. . . Ha. Ha.

Charlie Well you're in a shit mood.

Sam Sorry.

Charlie So did you get any food in?

Sam No.

Charlie So you've just been sitting around at home all day?

Act Two, Scene Three   77

Sam I've been working at home all day, yeah. Researching. For a paper. For work.

Charlie Alright, alright, sorry – Jesus.

Pause.

So, what do you want to do?

Sam What do you mean?

Charlie For food. What do you want to eat?

Sam I don't know. I haven't thought about it.

Charlie Well, do you want to think about it now?

Sam Fine.

Charlie Christ, you're no craic tonight. Work was shit, you know – not that you've asked – then I had to get home in *this* and I spend the whole day looking forward to coming back and seeing you and now you'll hardly say two words to me. That's just great.

Sam I'm sorry.

Charlie That's okay, that's okay.

Charlie's *tone shifts.*

So, what can we do to cheer you up, eh?

Sam I don't know.

Charlie *is physically closer to* **Sam** *now . . . maybe they try a touch, maybe a kiss.*

Sam *flinches away and re-establishes physical distance. Tense.*

There is a non-verbal dialogue to be found between them here.

The language of breath and bodies in space. Eye contact or no eye contact?

This takes as long as it takes.

Sam Get a Deliveroo if you want.

Charlie Okay. Okay, yeah. That'd be nice. Bit of takeaway, maybe stick something on Netflix. I don't get paid till Thursday though, so I'll put it on your card, yeah?

Sam No, don't. I don't want anything.

Charlie What? Oh, for fuck's sake.

Sam Well, I don't think it's fair that I keep paying for your shit.

Charlie Well, I don't think it's fair that you said you'd do a shop today and didn't.

Sam Right. A shop – which I would also have paid for, and you would have eaten most of.

Charlie Christ alright, I guess we're not eating then. I don't know why you're being such a cunt all of a sudden. You do realise it's completely crazy that you get in these moods out of nowhere and you expect me just to take it? I'm knackered. I've been at work all day.

Sam Are we ever going to talk about it?

Charlie Talk about what?

Sam It. The other night. It.

Charlie What's 'it'?

Sam I think we need to talk about it. I need us to talk about it.

Charlie *laughs.*

Charlie Are you tapped?

Sam Don't do that.

Charlie Do what?

Sam I've told you I hate it when you call me that.

Charlie Tapped?

Sam Tapped. Nuts. Crazy. Psycho. Any descriptor for a mentally ill person, basically.

Charlie Ah, Jesus. You know I don't mean it like that. It's a turn of phrase.

Sam It's not a turn of phrase.

Charlie It is, it's just something people say.

Sam Not to a person who – and it isn't. I don't know anyone else who calls anyone else that and it – I find it hurtful, you always telling me I can't trust myself.

Charlie What? That's a jump, Sam. That's totally out of the blue. I've never done that.

Sam You have. That I'm crazy and psycho and irrational and moody and I can't trust my own judgement because I'm mentally ill because of my 'fucked up childhood', like yours was so perfect, and –

Charlie Woah, woah, woah. Chill out. Chill. Seriously, I've never said any of that.

Sam No, not literally, not exactly, but you imply it. You make me feel like –

Charlie That's in your head, Sam.

Sam Like that! Stop it!

Charlie Oh my –

Sam This isn't the point anyway. It's. I want to talk about –

Charlie Yes. Right, 'it'. Sorry – sorry! Go on then, this mysterious 'it' –

Sam Don't do that. You know exactly what I'm talking about.

Charlie Okay great . . . It.

It, it, it, it it . . . hmm . . .

Sam The other night.

Pause.

I'd strained my neck again – and you said . . . you offered to . . . and then . . .

Pause.

I really need us to talk about it.

Charlie . . .

The – okay . . .

Sam I said no.

Long pause.

Charlie Right.

That.

Yeah.

Long pause.

Sam I didn't want –

Charlie I know.

Sam And you – you just – anyway.

Charlie Yeah.

Sam And then you just went to sleep.

Long pause.

And I haven't been able to stop thinking about it.

Scene Four

Sam's apartment. Evening.

An empty stage. The sound of keys in the front door and **Sam** *enters, followed closely by* **Charlie**. *They shed coats, bags etc as they speak.*

Sam Well, it was –

Charlie Mortifying, Sam. It was mortifying.

Sam No.

Charlie Humiliating.

Sam No. No, look, you're being –

Charlie '*I'm* being'? 'I'm being' what exactly?

Pause.

Sam Infantile.

Charlie Infantile?

Sam Infantile.

Charlie Infantile!

Sam Yes.

Charlie Fucking hell.

Pause.

Why can't you just say – say – 'you're being a big baby, Charlie?'

Sam What do you mean?

Charlie You're always trying to make me feel small. Talking down to me –

Sam I'm not.

Charlie – with your big words.

Sam I'm sorry, it's just – it's what came out, I didn't mean to –

Charlie You think you're better than me.

Sam I don't.

Charlie You want me to feel stupid.

Sam I don't think you're stupid, Charlie. I don't think that at all.

Charlie You were embarrassed to be with me. Tonight. I embarrass you.

Sam No.

Charlie They thought they were better than me.

Sam I don't think so.

Charlie I don't like your family, Sam.

Pause.

I'm sorry, but I don't. They're stuck up.

Pause.

You don't like them either.

Sam I do like them.

Pause.

I love them.

Charlie That's not the same thing.

You can love someone and you can not like them.

Sam Yes. Yes, I know . . . You can love someone and despise them, I'm not disputing that. You can really fucking hate the people you love sometimes.

Charlie I didn't ask for the thesis, Sam.

Sam Sorry?

Charlie You're doing it again. You drank too much.

Sam You drank more than I did.

Charlie I can handle it.

Sam And I do like them. I do! I am well aware that you can love someone and not like them, but I love them *and* I like them and – and I would really love it if you liked them too.

Charlie Well, they don't bring out a very nice side of you.

Sam That's . . . Oh. Ouch.

Charlie Also, this is how you feel when it suits you. When it's convenient and fun.

When it's dinner and drinks and they're ooh-ing and aah-ing over your latest list of achievements. But when I'm holding you up at four in the morning and you're choking on your vomit and crying and whining about your – what is it – your 'internalised trauma'. Again. Then it's a different story, isn't it?

Sam I think it's you that's not being very nice, Charlie.

Charlie Well, I think it's you that's being 'infan-ta-whatever-the-fuck'.

Pause.

Sam This can't all be about the bill, can it? Surely.

Charlie It was humiliating.

Sam It doesn't matter. No one cared.

Charlie They did. The way your cousin looked at me.

Sam Morgan is lovely. Morgan wouldn't think anything about – and Morgan also spent years sofa surfing and gigging and so, you know . . . understands that sometimes . . . when . . . I don't know where you've gotten this idea that my family are all . . . they're not materialistic . . . money doesn't . . .

Charlie It's ignorant, Sam. That's what it is.

Sam What's ignorant?

Charlie Assuming. Assuming that everyone can do that. Spending the evening ordering whatever you want – starters, sides, another bottle of wine, a round of after dinner fucking cocktails – and then saying that. 'Oh, we'll be splitting this between the six of us.' Just casually, like it's nothing, like it's obvious. Without asking anyone.

Sam It wasn't done with malice.

Charlie Do you know how it felt watching that card machine work its way round the table? Feeling everyone listening in when it got to our end?

Sam They weren't listening in.

Charlie *Everyone* heard you say it. 'The two of us on my card.' Everyone heard.

Sam But no one minded. No one minded at all.

Charlie It was humiliating.

Sam It's perfectly normal for a couple to pay on the same card! You could have gotten the last one, I could have owed you money for something –

Charlie But I hadn't. And you didn't.

Sam They didn't know that.

Charlie They did. It was humiliating.

Sam You're making a fuss over nothing.

Charlie It was a trap.

Sam What?

Charlie And it *was* intentional.

Sam I . . .

Charlie And it *was* malicious.

Act Two, Scene Four

Sam . . .

Charlie They wanted to show me that I don't fit in with them.

Sam . . .

Charlie That I don't fit with you.

Sam Charlie, that's ridiculous! We're not the fucking Rockefeller's –

Charlie I know.

Sam We're not – we're – I just have a normal family who don't –

Charlie Normal?

Sam I meant in terms of . . . financially speaking . . .

Look, they don't always go all out like that. It was an occasion.

Charlie It's not actually about the money, Sam. It's . . .

You just don't understand, I guess.

Sam I guess not.

Charlie You just can't see them the way I can.

Sam No.

Charlie You've got this massive blind spot with your whole family.

Sam Maybe.

Charlie There's just so much history there. Damage.

Sam Yeah.

Charlie And don't forget that this was an exception.

Sam . . . to?

Charlie You having a nice time with them tonight was an exception.

Sam Right.

Charlie And you know what they say . . .

Sam . . .?

Charlie Exception proves the rule.

Sam They do say that.

Charlie Yeah.

Sam Yeah . . .

Charlie I just want to protect you, Sam.

Sam Protect me?

Charlie Yeah. You're so perfect and fragile and brilliant and I wish I could just keep everything with the power to hurt you, just . . . you know . . . just . . . keep it over there. Away from you. Yeah?

Sam Charlie. That's sweet, but –

Charlie You can be a bit naive sometimes, Sam. Which is funny because you're so clever, but you haven't got . . . real . . . smarts, you know? People smarts.

Common sense.

Sam I guess.

Charlie But I do.

Sam Yeah.

Charlie Come here.

Charlie *opens arms wide and* **Sam** *steps into the embrace.*

Charlie Let's not fight.

Sam You're the one that was sulking all the way home.

Charlie I know, I know, you're right. I'm sorry. But you can see why now, yeah?

Sam I guess.

Charlie I was being a big baby, you were right.

Sam Yeah.

Charlie I'll make it up to you tomorrow.

Sam Oh yeah?

Charlie Yeah. I love you.

Sam I love you too.

88 Breaking

Scene Five

Sam's apartment. Day.

An empty stage. Then – a knock at the door.

Sam *enters from the bedroom and rushes to open it. It's* **Charlie**. *They embrace.*

Sam Oh, thank God!

Charlie Hey! Hey you!

Sam Thank God you're here, thank you. Thank you for coming.

Charlie Of course I came.

Sam I missed you.

Charlie I missed you too, so much. Are you okay now?

Sam Better, a bit better.

Charlie Good. Good. I was so worried about you. Here, sit down. Or, or lie.

Sam I'm feeling a lot better.

Charlie Good, but still. Relax. I want to look after you. Lie down here.

Sam Okay.

Charlie So what happened?

Sam I just got really faint, dizzy, and I thought I was going to be sick.

Charlie God.

Sam I wasn't though.

Charlie Good.

Sam But I just had to sit down. Right there in the, fucking, canned foods aisle. My knees went completely weak, and everything was spinning. So, I grabbed on to the trolly to, to steady myself – stupid – but the wheels were – you know – obviously – so. I just sat down. On the floor. In the aisle. Oh God, it was so embarrassing.

Charlie As long as you're alright.

Sam Yeah, right.

Charlie Have you drunk enough water? Since?

Sam Mmm. A bit. Probably not enough.

Charlie I'll get you some.

Sam I have a bottle by my bed, I'll get it.

Charlie I'll get it.

Sam I can get it, Charlie. But, thank you.

Sam *goes into the bedroom.*

Sam *returns with a bottle of water.*

Charlie Drink.

Sam I will.

Charlie Drink now.

Sam Okay, okay, drinking.

Sam *drinks.*

Thanks.

Sam *sits.*

Charlie So what happened after you sat down in the aisle?

Sam Someone asked me if I was okay. But I couldn't get any words out and then they – I think they went and got someone – a member of staff.

Charlie Right.

Sam Maybe they didn't get them, maybe the other person – the member of staff – maybe they were just in the aisle too. I was a bit out of it.

Charlie Yeah, of course.

Sam Anyway, they took me to the back, and I sat on a barrel thing for a bit.

Charlie Okay.

Sam No, not a barrel, a . . . a crate?

Charlie A crate, right, yeah.

Sam With my head between my legs.

Charlie Nice.

Sam Texted you –

Charlie Yeah.

Sam – as soon as I could focus on the screen properly. It, it wasn't so blurry then but I was still sure I was going to get sick. Everything was so, you know –

Charlie Poor Sammy.

Sam Anyway, because I could – you know – I was actually able to function a bit more at this point – able to use my phone at least – so, I got a taxi, on the app. I thought I was gonna throw up in the car. Get a fine.

Charlie God, yeah. Last thing you need. You poor thing.

Pause.

And you think it was a . . .?

Sam Yes. Yep. Just . . . just a panic attack, I think.

Charlie Like you . . .

Sam Like the ones I used to have. The ones I told you about. Yes.

Charlie And you're sure?

Sam So embarrassing.

Charlie You're sure we don't need to go to the hospital or anything? Just to be safe?

Sam I'm sure.

Charlie Okay.

Sam Once I got home and lay down for a bit it passed.

Charlie Good. I'm glad. I was so worried.

Sam I'm sorry that I worried you.

Charlie It's okay. I'm sorry I wasn't here sooner. I got here as fast as I could, but it's a long –

Sam I know. Yeah. You were right, getting in from yours is . . .

Charlie Yeah.

Sam Yeah.

Pause.

And – about that, actually . . . Errr. I actually . . .

I did want to talk to you about how we left things the other day.

I'm sorry. What I said wasn't fair.

Pause.

You were totally right. I have this lovely flat right in the centre and your place is . . . yeah . . . and with everything that's going on with your housemates at the moment, it's . . . Well, I get it.

Charlie Yeah?

Sam Yes, of course. Of course you can stay here. Whenever you need.

It makes sense.

Charlie That's . . . thank you.

And thank you for apologising.

Sam I was stressed. I was probably taking it out on you. Like you said.

Deadlines and. Stuff.

Charlie Yeah, I get it. It's okay. You work too hard.

Pause.

I . . .

Sam What?

Charlie Never mind.

Sam No, what is it?

Charlie I just want to be really clear. You know I can't . . . you know, chip in?

Or anything. Round here.

Sam Oh, right, I hadn't –

Charlie Just to keep things clear. I feel like I should be offering, and I'd love to, but . . . well, I'm barely managing the rent and the bills in my own place and –

Sam Right, of course.

Charlie – and you know that I don't have the same . . .

Sam Yes.

Charlie Income. As you. Right now.

Sam Absolutely.

Charlie And I can't ask my Dad again, it's just not fair on him.

Sam I . . . No, yeah . . . That's fine.

Pause.

Charlie Sam.

Sam Yeah?

Charlie You are amazing, and I love you. Now, please get some rest.

Sam Okay.

We should get you a key cut –

Sam's *phone starts ringing from another room.*

Oh, is that . . . Shit . . . Errr –

Charlie Stay!

Sam – Where did I leave my phone?

Charlie Stay right there. Don't move.

Charlie *exits to the bedroom.*

Sam (*calling through to* **Charlie**) Who is it?

The phone stops ringing.

Charlie *returns from the bedroom,* **Sam**'s *phone nowhere to be seen.*

Sam Charlie. Who was it?

Charlie It doesn't matter. Now. You need to relax.

Sam Who was it?

Pause.

Charlie.

Charlie She only upsets you.

Sam You need to stop doing that.

Charlie You need to get some rest.

Sam It's not your decision who I –

Charlie You have to admit that this time I'm justified.

Sam I – No. Maybe, but . . .

Charlie Sssh. Relax. Lie back.

Sam . . . Okay . . .

Charlie Chill. I'm calling in sick tomorrow.

Sam You don't have to.

Charlie To keep an eye on you. I want to.

Sam I'll be alright in the morning.

Charlie I don't care. I'm worried about you.

Sam Okay . . . if you're sure you won't get in –

Charlie I'll be your servant for the day. I'll wait on you hand and foot.

Sam Okay.

Charlie And I won't let you out of my sight.

Scene Six

Sam's apartment. The early hours of the morning.

Sam *and* **Charlie** *were out with friends tonight. They are very drunk. Music plays.*

They dance together. Then, **Charlie** *breaks away and stumbles to the sofa. Drinks.*

Sam *keeps dancing.* **Charlie** *keeps drinking, watching* **Sam**.

After some time, **Charlie** *stands again, wobbly, moving over to* **Sam** –

Charlie I fucking love you.

Sam I fucking love you.

Charlie *kisses* **Sam**.

Charlie You look amazing when you dance.

Sam *kisses* **Charlie**.

Charlie Majestic.

Sam *laughs.*

They kiss.

They wind their way back to the sofa, entangled.

The song comes to an end.

Sam Where did the music go?

Charlie Song finished.

Sam But why did it stop?

Charlie I said it ended, silly.

Sam It's on a playlist though.

Charlie Oh . . . Don't know then.

They laugh. They kiss.

Charlie You look great.

Sam You look great.

Charlie No, seriously, you look . . .

Hey, why did you have that big jumper on all night?

Sam I don't know. It's comfy and I was a bit cold. Why?

Charlie You should show off your body more when we go out.

Sam (*laughing*) Stop it. No, don't be silly.

Charlie I'm not, I'm serious. I love your body. You look . . .

Sam Great? You said that already.

Charlie I want everyone to see how lucky I am.

Sam Oh yeah?

Charlie Yeah. I'm going to dress you next time we go out. Alright?

Sam Dress me? You're going to dress me up like a doll?

Charlie Let me. Go on, it'll be fun.

Sam Dress me how?

Charlie Something tight. Something sexy. I want to show you off.

Sam That's not really me, Charlie . . .

Charlie It'll be fun.

Sam Okay, maybe. If you insist.

Charlie Tonight was fun.

Sam Yeah, it was.

Charlie Frankie was in good form.

Sam Yeah.

Act Two, Scene Six 97

Charlie I thought we got on well tonight.

Sam Me and you?

Charlie Me and Frankie.

Sam Oh. Yeah. Maybe.

Charlie Didn't you think?

Sam I didn't really notice either way, I wasn't paying much attention to Frankie.

Charlie Usually we don't.

Sam Get on?

Charlie No. I made a joke and Frankie laughed. At the bar.

Sam That's nice.

Charlie Yeah, it was good I think.

Sam I think you're overthinking it.

Charlie I'm saying it's a good thing.

Sam You're always thinking that you don't get on with people. Always thinking / that people don't like –

Charlie / Well, people don't like –

Sam – you! See!

Charlie They don't. Frankie doesn't.

Sam But, you just said –

Charlie Frankie likes you.

Sam Well, Frankie's my friend.

Charlie Frankie fancies you.

Sam Ugh, no. No. Shut up.

Charlie Of course Frankie fancies you, everyone fancies you.

Sam They don't.

Charlie But I get to have you.

Charlie *kisses* **Sam**.

Charlie More wine?

Sam Yeah. Thanks.

Charlie Uh-oh. Empty.

Sam Already. That was quick.

Charlie There's another bottle.

Sam Is there?

Charlie Yeah, we got one on the way home.

Sam Oh, yeah!

Charlie Go get the other bottle.

Sam Where is it?

Charlie Bedroom.

Sam Why's it in the bedroom? Where?

Charlie In my bag, remember?

Sam Oh. Right. Which bag?

Charlie Never mind. I'll get it.

Charlie *exits through the bedroom door.* **Sam** *sinks further into the sofa, drunkenly.* **Sam** *yawns, sleepiness setting in.*

Charlie *returns, triumphantly, with the new bottle of wine – makes a show of opening it and pouring out the two glasses, passing one to* **Sam**.

Sam Thank you.

They drink.

Charlie You should dance again.

Act Two, Scene Six 99

Sam There's no music.

Charlie Dance for me.

Sam Don't want to. I'm tired.

Charlie Alright.

Sam And my neck's all achy.

Charlie Again?

Sam I know. I keep straining it.

Charlie Well, you're always –

Sam Hunching over my laptop. Yeah, yeah, I know. I know.

Charlie Poor Sammy. You want a massage?

Sam Mmm, please. Yeah. In the morning. Too tired now.

Charlie No. Don't get sleepy yet.

Sam We've been up for hours.

Charlie But we haven't . . . *you know* . . . yet . . .

Sam Don't know if I want to.

Charlie Ah, that's not fair. You've got me in the mood.

Sam Oh yeah?

Sam *kisses* **Charlie**.

Charlie See, you do want to.

Sam No, I'm too tired. Maybe in a bit.

Charlie You'll fall asleep.

Sam I'm too drunk.

Charlie I just opened another bottle of wine.

Sam Sorry.

Charlie What do you want to do then?

Sam Cuddle.

Charlie Yeah?

Sam Talk.

Charlie What about?

Sam Something nice.

Charlie Something nice . . .

Sam Or. Tell me something you haven't told me before.

Charlie Hmmm . . . I love you?

Sam (*fake snore*) Boring. You're a broken record.

Charlie *laughs.*

Sam *snuggles into* **Charlie***'s chest.* **Charlie***'s arm wraps around.*

Charlie Hmmm . . .

Something else . . .

Pause. **Sam** *snuggles further in, eyes closing.*

Long pause.

And then . . .

Charlie When I was nine a kid in my class cornered me in the playground – called me all these names – and I pissed myself. And everyone saw.

Pause.

Sam*'s eyes open.*

Sam Really?

Charlie Really.

It's not something nice, but it is something I haven't told you before.

Sam Why did they do that?

Charlie I don't know. I didn't get on with other kids. They thought I was weird.

Sam I'm sorry that happened to you.

Charlie It's okay.

Sam I love you.

Charlie I love you too.

Pause.

Sam *snuggles back into* **Charlie**, *closing their eyes again.*

Sam My mum* used to call me names.

Charlie I know.

Pause.

Sam She didn't mean it though.

Charlie I know.

Pause.

Are you falling asleep?

Pause.

Sam?

Pause.

Sammy?

Sam Hmm?

Charlie Are you falling asleep?

Pause.

Sam *is asleep.*

* **'Mum'** *should be changed to 'Mam', 'Mom' etc according to what is natural for the actor.*

Scene Seven

Sam's apartment. Mid-morning.

Sam *sits at a desk working on a laptop, surrounded by papers and books.*

Charlie *emerges from the bedroom, not long awake, and stands in the doorway a moment, watching* **Sam** *at work.*

Charlie *pauses the video.*

Charlie Sam.

Sam *continues to work.*

Charlie Sam.

Sam *continues to work.*

Charlie Sammy . . .

Sam.

Sam Mmhmm.

Charlie Sam.

Sam Yeah, Charlie. I said yeah.

Charlie Do you still love me?

Pause.

Sam Yes.

Charlie Yeah. You sure?

Sam Yes, Charlie.

Charlie Good.

Pause.

Are you reeeaally / sure –

Sam Charlie, I'm working. I'm at work right now.

Charlie Sorry.

Charlie *moves over to the sofa, where they've left their iPad and headphones and lies down, sprawling out and stretching.* **Charlie** *puts the headphones on but the headphone jack dangles absent-mindedly as they search on YouTube and select a video.*

Charlie *presses play on the video.*

Still not noticing that the headphones aren't plugged in, **Charlie** *increases the volume.*

Some time passes.

Sam　You know those headphones aren't plugged in.

Charlie, *attention on the video, hasn't heard this. Laughs at the screen.*

Sam　Could you maybe turn it down a bit?

Charlie　Huh?

Charlie *finally notices that the headphones are dangling –*

Oh! Ha.

– plugs them in and continues enjoying the video.

Pause.

Sam　When do you leave for work?

Pause.

Charlie.

Pause.

(*Louder.*) Charlie, when are you leaving?

Charlie *pauses the video and removes the headphones.*

Charlie　What, Sammy?

Sam　Errr. When are you off to work?

Charlie　Oh. Two thirty, two forty-five ish.

Sam *checks the time.*

Sam Right.

Pause. They smile at each other.

Charlie *is about to return to the video, when –*

Sam I wish you wouldn't ask me that all the time.

Charlie Ask you what?

Sam If I love you.

Charlie If you said it more I wouldn't have to.

Sam I tell you I love you all the time.

Charlie I tell you I love you more.

Sam That's – I say it a normal amount.

Charlie So, what? I love you too much?

Sam That's not – no. Just – I – ah. Never mind.

Charlie You're pretty mean to me, sometimes. But I do love you.

Sam . . . No, I'm not?

Charlie Only joking.

Sam Okay. I don't think I . . . I mean, I'm sorry. If you feel like I . . .

Charlie Go on, get back to work. You're cute when you're concentrating.

Sam *half turns back to their work. Suddenly remembers –*

Sam Wait. But I thought you were working a mid-shift today?

Charlie Half three till close.

Sam I thought – I'm sure you said it was earlier?

Charlie Nope, half three till close.

Sam Right . . .

Charlie Why? You want to get rid of me?

Sam No, no. I just – I thought that was why you had to stay over last night.

Charlie I didn't have to, I wanted to spend time with you.

Sam I really do have to get this done today.

Charlie Finish it when I go in.

Sam It doesn't really work like that.

Charlie You're freelance, it doesn't matter when you do it as long as it's done.

Sam Maybe that's . . . technically true. But . . . Well, just because I *can* work any time doesn't mean I want to. I like routine and structure and – solitude. I work better when I work under the right circumstances.

Time of day, environment. It all makes a really big difference.

Charlie That sounds like a lot of fancy ways of saying 'fuck off Charlie'.

Sam No, no! Honestly, I promise.

Charlie You could take a long lunch. From now until I go. Then work a couple of extra hours this evening. You'll still get it all done.

Sam I want to do it now. My . . . my brain's used to working / at this –

Charlie That's in your head, you know.

Sam Yes, actually. It is. It's psychology. Science. And it's evidence based.

My energy is better now. I've done my morning routine, I've done my starting rituals and all of that tells my brain that, that it's / time to –

Charlie Sounds like a load of shit.

Sam It helps me.

Charlie Just do all that on the days that I'm not here, then.

Sam You're always here.

Charlie Start it when I go to work.

Sam I work best in the mornings –

Charlie Do it when I'm at mine.

Sam My work is important to me, Charlie –

Charlie You just don't want to spend time with me.

Sam – and you're never at yours anymore.

Pause.

Charlie Is that a problem?

Pause.

Sam No.

Pause.

Charlie Have I annoyed you?

Sam No.

Charlie I have.

Sam No, no, you're fine.

Charlie I have. I have, I've annoyed you. Great. Sorry.

Sam No, please don't get upset. I'm sorry.

Pause.

I'm sorry, Charlie.

Charlie.

You haven't annoyed me.

Come here.

Act Two, Scene Seven   107

Charlie *comes to* **Sam**.

Sam *embraces* **Charlie**.

Sam I'm sorry if I hurt your feelings. I love you.

Charlie I love you too, Sammy Sam.

They embrace for a moment. Then –

I've got an idea!

Sam Charlie, I really do need to –

Charlie No, no, no, shush. Ssssh. Here. Look. Let's put this away. Please.

Charlie *shuts the laptop.*

Sam Charlie!

Charlie Please, Sam. Don't argue. Please. No more arguing.

Just this once? Please. Please . . .?

Look, you deserve a break! And I am – I'm being a pain in the arse and I'm going to make up for it. It's not going to happen every day, but just for today, please, I want to make it up to you. I want to. I want to . . . make you a great-big-fuck-off-brunch.

Sam Charlie, I don't . . .

Charlie Sam. I insist. I was being annoying, I get it. I know. I was being . . .

I've been hanging about all day, lounging around in your apartment, making a mess, taking up space, doing sweet fuck all and the absolute least I can do is treat you to a nice meal once in a while.

Right? So. What have you got in?

Sam Umm –

Charlie Eggs? Have you got eggs?

Sam *nods.*

Charlie Good. Tomatoes? Avocado?

Sam Yeah.

Charlie And your favourite – smoked salmon?

Sam There's a bit left in that pack, yeah. Not much. But –

Charlie Well, I'll put the salmon in yours then, yeah?

I'll cook it right into the scrambled eggs, just the way you like it. Yeah?

Sam Thanks.

Charlie Why don't you nip over to that place you love, the one across the road? Get us some proper coffees to have with it. You'd like that wouldn't you? And get some air. I think some air would do you good, wouldn't it? And I'll get cooking.

Sam Yeah. Okay. But – . . . Okay.

Charlie Okay. Coat.

Charlie *holds out the coat and helps* **Sam** *into it.*

Sam Thanks.

Charlie Kiss?

They kiss.

Love you.

Sam I love you too.

Charlie Oat milk cappuccino.

Sam I know.

Sam *leaves.*

Epilogue

This should feel, at first, like a continuation of the previous scene. Then, perhaps, like the worlds of all the **Sam**'s *and all the* **Charlie**'s *are bleeding into each other for a moment. Or, perhaps, like the non-naturalistic and unapologetically theatrical world – the world in which this play is being performed in this space at this time – is suddenly imposing itself upon the realities the character/s are experiencing in the scene.*

Charlie (*whoever has been playing* **Charlie** *in Act 2, Scene 7*) *is left alone onstage.*

Silence.

Perhaps the lights flicker.

Perhaps the normal sounds of the room heighten or increase to a slow crescendo, for example: a clock ticking, the hum of a fridge, the dishwasher cycle ending.

Silence.

Charlie *looks to the door that* **Sam** *last walked through.*

Charlie Sam.

Sam?

We hear keys in the front door, the one that **Charlie** *is looking at.*

Another Charlie *enters through the door.*

Charlie *and the* **Other Charlie** *do not see or hear each other.*

Other Charlie *looks around for evidence of* **Sam**. *Moves towards the bedroom calling –*

Other Charlie Sam.

Charlie Sammy.

Other Charlie Sam?

Sam *enters through the bedroom door.*

Sam *can see and be seen by the* **Other Charlie**, *but not* **Charlie**.

Sam Mmhmm.

Other Charlie Sam.

Another Sam *comes to stand in the (still open) front door.*

Other Sam Yeah, Charlie. I said yeah.

Charlie / Other Charlie Do you still love me?

Pause.

Sam / Other Sam Yes.

Other Charlie Yeah?

Charlie You sure?

Sam Yes, Charlie.

The Other Sam *nods reluctantly.*

Charlie Good.

Blackout.

Acknowledgements

I'd like to say a huge thank you to everyone that supported me in the writing and development of *Breaking* (originally titled *Breaking Point Blank*), my first play.

Firstly, I'd like to thank Seda Ilter and Rebecca Mairs who asked me the right questions when it was still just an idea; William Ellis who supported me as the play took shape and helped me to believe in its potential; Rían Smith, Selina O'Reilly, Caitríona McLaughlin and Conor McPherson for their interest and encouragement; all the actors who read Sam and Charlie during the many formal or informal development sessions, every single one of you taught me something new about these characters and my own words – Tia Dunn, Ian Millar, Winnie Ikediashi, Mickey Knighton, Sophia Mastrosavaki, Michael Bucke, Meadhbh Maxwell, Benedict Landsbert-Noon, Graeme Dalling, Scarlet Hunter, Roei Cohen, Luiza Válio, Sam Labovitz, Domhnall Herdman, Caoimhe Coburn Gray, Patrick Martins, Kate Gilmore, Cillian Lenaghan, Liz FitzGibbon – and, of course, the four actors originating the roles Eavan Gaffney, Curtis-Lee Ashqar, Matthew Malone and Jeanne Nicole Ní Áinle.

I'd also like to give a huge thank you to Bloomsbury and Callan McCarthy for publishing my very first play, not to mention particularly emphatic thanks to Jim Culleton, Gavin Kostick and Laura MacNaughton for wanting to produce it, and to the whole team working on Fishamble's premier production for the Dublin Theatre Festival.

Finally, I'd like to thank all the tutors and staff at The Lir Academy, where I trained as an actor, my agent Holly Carey, my friends, my parents (all four of you) and my partner Barry.